# NIGHTMARE....

*Vicki dreamed she was in some cold, frightening place from which there was no escape. A dreadful blackness shut her in. Round and round she turned, but there was no way out, only endless rows of windows and closed doors. Suddenly she knew she was in the harem, and all around in the darkness were ghosts from the long ago past, whispering.*

She *must* get out—she must wake up! She knew this was a nightmare, and she had only to open her eyes to be rid of it. But the crushing darkness, the sounds of rain, the whispering within, were clear and real.

Suddenly she knew the truth. This was no dream. She *was* awake. She was alone in the middle of the night, and something was moving toward her in the darkness. . . .

# Mystery of the Golden Horn

*by Phyllis A. Whitney*

A SIGNET BOOK

NEW AMERICAN LIBRARY

TIMES MIRROR

Library of Congress Catalog Card Number: 62-13874

This is an authorized reprint of a hardcover edition
published by The Westminster Press.

 SIGNET TRADEMARK REG. U.S. PAT. OFF. AND FOREIGN COUNTRIES
REGISTERED TRADEMARK—MARCA REGISTRADA
HECHO EN CHICAGO, U.S.A.

SIGNET, SIGNET CLASSICS, MENTOR, PLUME AND MERIDIAN BOOKS
are published by The New American Library, Inc.,
1301 Avenue of the Americas, New York, New York 10019

FIRST PRINTING, JULY, 1974

4 5 6 7 8 9

PRINTED IN THE UNITED STATES OF AMERICA

For Nurcihan Kesim,
who showed me what Turkish hospitality
was like and became my good friend.
Gratefully, affectionately

# Contents

# 1

# The Broken Pieces

Vicki Stewart sat huddled in the darkness at the turn of the stairway. Her pajama-clad knees were pulled up to her chin, her hands clasped tensely around them. Brown hair, short and curly at the temples, was tousled, since she had left her bed for this eavesdropping, and her dark brows were drawn into a scowl as she strained to listen.

Downstairs in the living room, the four aunts were holding what they called a "council of war." They were talking about her, and Vicki knew if she listened long enough she would undoubtedly hear some very unpleasant things. When they turned unpleasant enough, she would run softly downstairs in her bare feet and burst dramatically in upon them. She would glare at them all and make her announcement loudly and firmly. "No!" she would cry. "I will *not* be sent off to Istanbul! I *won't* go to Turkey, and you can't make me!"

Her heart thumped as she imagined their reaction. She was so warm with anger, so trembly with anticipation, that she could hardly hear what was being said. Yet she must hear in order to understand the plans that were being made for her.

There—that was Aunt Laura speaking. She was the oldest of the three who were her mother's older sisters, and she was the one Vicki liked the least.

"Thank goodness Alan has come to his senses and is willing to take her!" Aunt Laura boomed. "Let me have his letter, May, if you've read it. He says we can send her to Istanbul as soon as she has her passport and all the right shots."

"It's the only solution, of course," Aunt Connie said. "We have planned our round-the-world tour for months, and we can't cancel it at the last minute because of this accident, unhappy as we feel about it."

The accident had been a dreadful fall down the basement stairs by Vicki's mother. It had sent her to the hospital with a damaged back and brought on the whole crisis. As Vicki knew very well, no one felt worse about this than Mother.

"Of course, we can't cancel the trip," Aunt Gertrude echoed. She was the one who always agreed with Laura and Constance.

The rustle of paper told the listener on the stairs that her father's letter was being passed from aunt to aunt. Vicki had to blink to keep back the furious tears. If she meant to confound and defy the aunts, it would never do to start weeping out of sheer rage. She would *not* go to Turkey. This was only April. There were two months left of the spring term. Margie's birthday party was coming up next month, and there were other events she didn't want to miss. When school ended she would go off to Camp Glenwood with the other girls as usual.

A voice much gentler than Aunt Laura's, and not nearly so firm, was speaking, and Vicki listened again. That was Aunt May, her father's sister, the only one of the aunts who lived in this house and had taken charge of things since Mother's fall.

"I wonder—" Aunt May began hesitantly, "—do you suppose we might take Vicki with us on the trip?"

Aunt Laura's disgusted snort was the answer. "Don't be a ninny, May. Do you think we want that spoiled, sulky child ruining a trip we've looked forward to and are spending a good deal of money for? Her father has settled the matter. She will go to Turkey, and that is that."

This was the moment. Vicki dared wait no longer. With her heart thudding in her ears, she tore down the stairs and flung herself into the living room. If everything hadn't been so desperate and tragic, she might have laughed at the shocked expressions on the four aunts' faces.

"I won't go to Turkey!" she shouted. The words came out much louder than she intended, but she kept right on. "I won't! I won't! I know you all hate me and don't want me around, but I won't go to Turkey."

Aunt Laura recovered first. "Control yourself, Victoria," she snapped. "Little girls who eavesdrop are unlikely to hear much that is favorable said about them. Of course you will go to Turkey. You have nothing to say about it, actually. Please take that scowl off your face and get back to bed where you belong."

Aunt May said, "Oh, Vicki dear—" helplessly and fell silent.

"I can't leave school before the term is over. You ought to know that," Vicki said rudely, marshaling her arguments.

The eldest of the aunts snorted through her nose again. "Perhaps I'd better tell you something, Victoria. It is unfortunate that it must be broken to you like this, but I had a long talk with your teacher and with the principal of your school two days ago. You are failing in all your subjects but one, and there's not the faintest chance of your being promoted at the end of the term. Mr. Albright says it will be necessary for you to stay behind and take the year over."

"Oh no!" Aunt May cried in alarm. "Vicki is such a bright girl—she couldn't possibly fail."

"Not bright enough to work at her studies and make a passing grade," Aunt Laura said. "This is going to be a fine thing to report to her father, who is undoubtedly a brilliant man, even though a bit eccentric."

Vicki said nothing at all. The hot anger was seeping away, leaving in its place a queer, cold lump in the pit of her stomach. She knew things hadn't been going well in school for some time. She couldn't remember exactly how far back it was that things had started changing, but somewhere she had got off on a wrong foot. Then had come that scrape she and some of the other girls had become involved in and for which she had been blamed as the leader. Certainly it had been her idea to climb in a window and explore that empty old house on Hillcrest Road, and the others had been willing enough to follow her. Only it hadn't been empty, and the woman who had just moved in as caretaker had trapped them upstairs and had phoned the police. They hadn't done any real damage, but there had been some vandalism around town, and this caused an uproar.

A lot of people had been critical of Victoria Stewart. She was clearly a difficult girl who got other people's daughters in trouble. There had been headshaking among some of the teachers at school, and Aunt Laura had a conniption. Afterward, it had been hard to think about lessons, and suddenly Vicki hadn't cared any more. What Aunt Laura had just revealed wasn't really a surprise. A shock, yes, but not a surprise. Mr. Albright had seen it coming. He had even had a talk with Mother once or twice. Vicki had promised to improve, and Mother had not told the aunts or even written to Dad about it. Yet Vicki had not buckled down to work. The wrong foot, once started, kept right on putting itself forward.

Now the worst had happened—the thing she had in some queer way been daring to happen. And it felt quite awful. To fail—to be the only one of the whole class left behind while her friends went on—that was too dreadful to contemplate. Everyone was against her, and nothing was much use any more.

The aunts rustled among themselves, "tsk-tsking" furiously—all except soft-hearted Aunt May, who had begun to dab at her eyes with a handkerchief and to sniffle softly.

"I see what I must do," she said between sniffles, and the other three stopped whispering and stared at her. "I'll give up the trip and stay home with Vicki. Then perhaps she can work hard this last month or so, and she won't have to be sent off to Turkey, where she doesn't want to go. After all, I'm not a very good sailor. I'm sure to get seasick and—"

The other three aunts pounced on her indignantly. They told her she was to stop making a door mat of herself, that an ungrateful child like Victoria was not worth such a sacrifice, and, of course, she would go on the trip. She had been looking forward to it more than any of them, and they wouldn't listen to such nonsense.

Vicki swallowed hard over the cold lump that now seemed to be wedged in her throat. She stammered a little when she spoke and hated the sign of her own weakness. The one thing she didn't want the aunts to guess was how awful she felt.

"M-m-maybe I c-c-could stay with Margie until Mother is well again. Or till I can go to camp. Margie's mother—"

"Do you think Margie's mother would take such a responsibility?" Aunt Laura demanded. "Do you think any mother in this town would put up with you for more than an overnight visit? You used to be a nice enough child, but you've been changing lately. I might tell you, young lady, that there are mothers in this town who don't think you are a good influence for their daughters. That last scrape when you led Margie and the others into—"

"Don't," Aunt May pleaded. "Don't scold her now. Vicki dear, Istanbul must be a fascinating city, and your father writes that there's another girl your age in the house where you'll stay. Adria March, a girl whose mother is from this very town—"

"That witch-girl!" Aunt Laura broke in. "I saw the child a couple of years ago when her parents brought her home on a visit. She's probably worse than ever now, what with her father and mother killed in—"

Aunt May stood up with more firmness than she usually displayed. "That's quite enough," she said. "Can't you see how Vicki feels? Not one of us has a child of her own, but at least I can remember what it was like to be young. I can remember how much it hurts sometimes to be young. Please go home now, all of you. Vicki's father has decided what must be done, and Vicki and I want to talk it over. Come upstairs, dear."

Aunt May held out a cool, thin hand and took hold of Vicki's perspiring fingers. In spite of all the things she longed to say, in spite of wanting to tell the aunts off once and for all, Vicki found herself climbing the stairs beside

Aunt May, holding tightly to her hand as she had done when she was small and worried about crossing streets.

At the top of the stairs, Aunt May put an arm around her shoulders, and they went into Vicki's bedroom. It was a pretty room, with yellow primrose wallpaper and a view that looked out upon a weeping willow tree and the river beyond—a view she would have to give up for some dreadful faraway place where people didn't even speak her language and where she had no friends.

She felt too limp, however, to struggle any more. The only thing she wanted was to get to her mother, to have Mother's arms safely and reassuringly about her, to know that someone loved her, no matter what. But Mother was out of reach and not to be worried. Her father ... Thinking of Dad made everything worse. As Aunt Laura had said, he was a very brilliant man and occupied with his own work and interests. It seemed as though she had been on better terms with him when she was little than she was now. Because of his teaching, most of the young people he knew were of college age, and he didn't have much in common with a twelve-year-old. He would never, never understand how a daughter of his could fail in school. Facing her father would be the hardest thing of all.

Aunt May turned on a yellow-shaded lamp that matched the wallpaper. It had been a present from Mother last Christmas. When she had tucked Vicki into bed, she sat down with Dad's letter in her hand.

"Just think," she said, trying hard to sound sprightly and bright, "Your father is living in the old house of a Turkish pasha. This American woman, Mrs. Byrne, whose husband is a civil engineer, has taken over this fascinating house and is running it as a pension—a sort of boarding-house—for Americans."

Aunt May was trying so hard that Vicki felt a little sorry for her. After all, none of this was Aunt May's fault, and she had been willing to give up her trip around the world in order to help.

"What's a pasha?" Vicki asked, though she didn't really care.

"A pasha—let's see now. I'm not quite sure. Wait a minute till I get the dictionary from my room."

She hurried off, leaving a whiff of violet perfume behind her. Vicki closed her eyes and lay very still. She couldn't bear facing the kids at school, once they knew. Not even Margie, who wasn't awfully clever, but would have no trouble passing. While she, Vicki Stewart, who had the most enterprising ideas and was looked up to by quite a few people—*she*— Oh, it didn't bear thinking about. But how could she stop when her thoughts were seething and the pain of coming disgrace stabbed through her like the beginning of a very bad toothache?

Aunt May came hurrying back with the big dictionary in her arms.

"Here you are," she said, plumping it down on the bed. "Listen to this. '*Pasha*: Formerly, an honorary title, placed after the name, given to officers of high rank in Turkey, as to governors of provinces, military commanders, etc. There were three classes of pashas, whose rank was formerly distinguished by one, two, or three horsetails borne on their standards, three tails marking the highest rank.' Isn't that interesting? I wonder if this pasha had three horsetails. On his standard, that is."

Vicki couldn't have cared less, but Aunt May looked as thought she might begin to cry in earnest, and then Vicki's own tears would never hold back.

"What did Aunt Laura mean about that girl being a witch?" she asked.

Aunt May drew a long, sniffling breath, dabbed at her eyes, and tried to control her emotion.

"Oh, you know Laura. She doesn't understand young people very well. Adria seemed an attractive girl to me. You didn't meet her because you were away at camp. But her mother and your mother were very dear friends when they were young. In fact, it was Adria's father who was teaching art in Turkey and persuaded your father to come out to join the staff at the girls' college. It was tragic when both Adria's father and mother were killed in a mountaineering accident in Switzerland. They were caught by an avalanche, I believe. It happened only last year. I don't quite know how Adria happens to be staying on in Tur-key with Mrs. Byrne."

"But why did Aunt Laura use a word like 'witch' about her?" Vicki persisted.

Aunt May closed her eyes, trying to remember. "I re-call that there was something a little strange about Adria. Of course, she was only ten at the time I saw her. She of-ten seemed to be thinking of something else, as if she were in a daydream way off from everyday affairs. And she had a way of walking, of running—almost as if she floated. Such a graceful little thing. I remember the way she laughed too. It sounded like a silver flute." Aunt May broke off as if she found herself wandering too far afield, and wound up rather lamely, "I'm sure she's a pleasant girl, and you two will be good friends."

Vicki doubted this. She did not think at the moment that she would ever have any friends at all, ever again.

"Turkey!" she said, and somehow her unhappiness, her despair, got into the very sound of the word. "Men in fezes with dozens of wives in veils. And no camp. No fun all summer. No Margie. Nothing." She did not mention being cut off from Mother, which was the worst thing of all.

"I don't think Turkey is quite like that any more," Aunt May said. "Since Alan, your father, went out there, I've been reading about it. And I've studied the map of Istanbul that he sent home." She went to the table where Vicki's neglected schoolbooks were stacked and got a pad and pencil. "Look, dear, here is a sketch of the way the city sprawls across two worlds."

She began to draw rapidly on the paper, and as she drew, she talked, becoming a little excited about her own words.

"You know, Istanbul—they used to call it Constantino-ple—is a city where Europe and Asia meet. The two con-tinents come together at this strait that is the Bosporus. All this squiggly gray part I've marked in is Istanbul and its suburbs. The school where your father teaches is a very famous college up here on the European side of the Bosporus where I've put an $x$. And here's another fascinating thing about the city, Vicki: Look at the way it strad-dles another waterway that divides old Istanbul from the newer part. This inlet is the famous Golden Horn, with two bridges across it, connecting the two parts of the city. I can almost see what it must be like. Perhaps I'll see it too on this trip we're taking."

Mention of the trip brought her attention back to Vicki, and she looked sad again.

"I wish I could help, dear. I know how painful this must be for you. I wish Laura—"

"It doesn't matter," Vicki said.

At least Aunt May wouldn't remind her that if only she had worked harder ... That was the dreadful thing—the fact that it was absolutely too late, that what was done was so thoroughly done that nothing could now be changed. It was like breaking up a part of her life.

Vicki propped herself up in bed on one elbow and reached out to Aunt May. "Do I have to go back to school tomorrow? Please, can't we hurry about getting me off to Turkey? So—so I won't have to explain a lot of things that will be—hard to explain?"

"Oh, dear," Aunt May said. "I'm not sure. I ought to consult—" Then she took Vicki's hand firmly. "No—I won't consult anyone. Your mother is too ill, and your aunts would only object. I'll—make the decision myself. You may drop out of school now, Vicki. Under the cir-cumstances, I don't suppose it will matter. Tomorrow we'll see about your passport and what shots you need, and start getting your clothes ready. Will that suit you, dear?"

Vicki nodded, her eyes blurry. Nothing mattered a great deal, but to escape was of some help. Aunt May leaned over and kissed her cheek.

"Will you be all right now, dear? You won't walk about? I mean—"

"In my sleep?" Vicki said. "I don't think so."

This was something she used to do when she was little, but the only time she had done it recently was the night after Mother had been taken to the hospital and no one knew how bad her injuries might be.

Aunt May turned out the light. "Go to sleep, Vicki dear. And dream about the city on the Golden Horn. Sleep late in the morning—there's no need now to get up early."

*No need now*—the words seemed to echo after her as Aunt May closed the door.

Vicki lay in the soft spring darkness, listening to the whisper of the newly green willow tree that had lulled her to sleep for as long as she could remember. But she did not think of the willow or of Istanbul. She thought only of broken pieces of her life that could not be mended. So needlessly broken—that was the awful part. She knew perfectly well that she wasn't a stupid girl, nor even a lazy one.

Suddenly she was filled with a disliking that shook her and brought stormy tears. Not disliking for her teachers or Mr. Albright, not for Aunt Laura or her two sisters, but only for Vicki Stewart who had brought disgrace upon herself and must now run away to hide in a foreign land.

I must go to sleep, she told herself. Only in sleep would there be forgetfulness. But it was hard to sleep when her world had turned upside down, and she didn't know how to pick up any of the pieces.

# 2

# Meeting in Istanbul

Only the breathless rush of the following days made them possible to endure. No one had to be told now about her failure in school, and Vicki managed to put on enough of a performance so that not even her best friends suspected what she was suffering inside. She told them she didn't want to go to Istanbul and let that account for her lack of excitement about the things that were happening to her.

A week before she left, a letter came from her father. When she was alone she read it over and over and did not show it to Aunt May or to her mother in the hospital.

He wrote about how beautiful Turkey was and what a fascinating time she would have in Istanbul—but he didn't explain these terms so that she could see and hear and taste and touch what he was telling her. "Beautiful Istanbul" meant nothing at all. The one interesting thing he mentioned in his letter, he didn't elaborate on. In one place he said, "You'll be interested to know that there's a castle near where we are living," and let it go at that.

Apparently he remembered the collection of castle pictures she had started when she was younger and still kept up whenever she found one to cut from a magazine. It might be fun to visit a real castle.

In another paragraph he had started to write something about Adria March and then scratched it out as though he'd changed his mind. Following the scratched out part he wrote: "Adria is having a bad time recovering from the shocking loss of her parents. Mrs. Byrne is a distant cousin, I believe, and is taking care of her for the time being. I'm afraid this is rather a burden for her. Her husband is a civil engineer and away a good deal of the time, working on the building of new roads in Turkey. They have a son, Kenneth, who is about six months older than you are. I'm afraid he doesn't get along very well with Adria, but I hope you and Ken will be friends."

All this was baffling, and when it was added to what Aunt Laura and Aunt May had said about Adria March, it made an odd picture. Vicki had a feeling that she wasn't going to like Adria any more than Ken did. About Ken, she would have to wait and see.

Dad concluded with a paragraph that warned her of the fact that it was difficult to have her come to Istanbul without her mother. She would be pretty much in Mrs. Byrne's charge, and he hoped she would do her best to be nice to everyone. He said nothing at all about her failure in school, though Aunt Laura had written him airmail concerning it, and he must have known the worst by the time he wrote this letter.

In any case it was a letter she found herself resenting. Especially that last paragraph. Why couldn't he take it for granted that she would do her best and behave well, instead of hinting that she might not and warning her that she wasn't really welcome? She began to "dig in her heels"—as Aunt Laura called it—in resistance against her father and everything connected with Istanbul.

The worst part of leaving came when she said good-by to her mother. Aunt May took her to the hospital that day and left her alone in the two-bed room where her mother lay beside the window, looking pale and weak. It broke her heart to have Mother trying so hard to make the best of things when she was in pain and so terribly discouraged as well. At least it was helpful that her mother didn't know about her failure at school.

"It's a shame that I had to spoil all our plans with that silly fall," she said. "It would have been much nicer if you and I could have gone to Istanbul together next year, as we'd planned to do when your father was sure he wanted to stay on at this teaching post in Turkey. At least the doctor was not altogether discouraging today. He said I seem to be mending well—so who knows, perhaps you'll see me there before you expect me."

Vicki could not place much hope in her words. She had heard the grave way the doctor had discussed her mother's case with Aunt May. There was the very real possibility that she might be an invalid for some time to come, even when she left the hospital. A nurse would come home with her and take care of her for a time at least, and a trip to Istanbul seemed out of the question.

Before Vicki left the hospital, her mother spoke of Adria—or at least she spoke of how fond she had been of Adria's mother and how she had grieved over her death. They had been best friends when they were Vicki's age and all through high school and college. It was a tragic loss for Adria, and Vicki must be very kind to her.

There it was again—"Be nice, be kind." Words that somehow rubbed her the wrong way, even from Mother, and made her want to be anything but nice.

All too soon, visiting hours were up, and Vicki fought unsuccessfully to hold back her tears. Telling Mother good-by was like cutting herself off from all love and comfort and reassurance. All the way home on the bus she was silent and prickly and not very nice to her aunt. She had a horrid feeling inside that she wanted to hurt others as much as she was being hurt—though she knew that made no sense at all.

On the day of her departure, all four of the aunts put her on the plane to New York. Vicki felt like a doll that was being handed about and made to do all sorts of things without any will of her own.

Then a pretty, smiling stewardess took her in charge, and she boarded the plane with other passengers.

All through the trip the stewardesses were kind to her, and so were some of the other passengers. Though faces changed when she was transferred to a jet in New York, everyone seemed anxious to look out for her and make her trip pleasant.

New impressions began to come so fast that everything

blurred together. She slept and ate and slept again. They touched down at London, at Frankfurt, at Munich, and time ceased to have any meaning since it changed constantly as they flew east to meet the sun.

Sometimes on the way she thought about Dad, and her memory played her a queer trick. Though he had been gone from home for less than a year, she could not remember exactly how he looked or how he sounded. She could remember only a sense of sternness about him, when she did not measure up to his expectations. Not that he scolded. But he would go off and shut himself away with his work, as though he put her completely out of his mind. If this happened in Turkey, what was she to do?

The trip was nearly over now, and a stewardess leaned toward her and pointed to the window. "That's the Sea of Marmara down there on your right. We're flying over Eastern Thrace now—the name they give to Turkey-in-Europe. Our flight is quite late, I'm afraid, but I'm sure your father will meet you. Don't worry about a thing."

Vicki managed a stiff smile. Don't worry about a thing? Yet all she could do was worry—not about those matters which seemed to concern the stewardess, but about the look she would find on her father's face when she first saw him. It would be a look that would tell her he knew that Alan Stewart's daughter had not made a passing grade in school.

When they left the plane at Istanbul, another passenger helped her, and just as Vicki's suitcase was cleared, a young woman in uniform came to say that Miss Stewart's friends were waiting and she could come right along. Somehow that did not sound reassuring, and Vicki followed her uncertainly toward the waiting room. Clearly her father wasn't there. Instead, an American woman and a boy came forward to greet her.

The woman was large and breezy of manner. She held out her hand in a way that did not concentrate on Vicki—as if she was thinking of something else as she shook hands.

"I'm Mrs. Byrne," she said. "And this is my son Kenneth. Your father had an important appointment in town this afternoon, and since your flight was so late, he couldn't meet your plane as he intended. Is that all your baggage? Do lend a hand, Ken. And let's hurry—we've a long drive home."

Vicki handed the heavier bag to Ken. She still felt breathless and a little confused, simply from coming so far so fast. She couldn't even be sure whether she was hurt or only relieved over the fact that her father had not come to meet her, and the moment she dreaded still lay ahead.

As they walked outside, she stole a glance at Kenneth Byrne. He was taller than she and quite good-looking, with carroty hair and lots of freckles. His eyes were bright blue, and there was a teasing look about them that matched his grin when he caught her looking at him. He carried her suitcase easily as he followed his mother with an eary stride. Vicki had trouble keeping up with the two long-legged Americans.

When they reached the small English car, Ken put the bags in the trunk and opened the door for Vicki to sit in the back seat. He sat up in front with his mother.

Daylight was fading as they followed the highway through rolling Turkish countryside. As she drove, Mrs. Byrne asked questions that were easy enough to answer—about the plane trip, about Vicki's mother and home.

"It's too bad your father couldn't meet you," she went on in her offhand way. "You know he's making a study of Turkish wall ceramics, and the man he had to see is down from Ankara just for today. But he'll be home for dinner tonight. Adria couldn't come either. She's in bed with a cold. You know about Adria, I suppose? I'm afraid she's having a difficult time right now. Sometimes I hardly know what to do about her. I'll admit that I've had more experience raising boys than girls. Ken has two grown-up brothers back in the States."

The red-haired boy looked around from his place in the front seat. "Adria is a crazy one," he said.

"Don't talk like that," his mother chided and changed the subject. "Do you see those walls ahead of us, Vicki?

They're the old land walls of Istanbul—built to protect the city on the land side. Hundreds of years old they are."

By now the sun was setting, but Vicki could see the crumbling walls stretching out to right and left of the gap where the road cut through, the line broken by thick towers that had once been square but were now disintegrating into rubble.

Ken had no interest in the walls. "That was sure a nutty thing Adria did yesterday, Mom. Out in the rain like that!"

"Never mind, dear," his mother said. "She's paying for it by having to stay in bed today. I'm sure Vicki will be good for Adria. She needs another girl in the house."

Ken snorted impolitely but did not explain the reason for his doubt. Vicki began to feel a certain sympathy for the odd, mysterious Adria. It was rather novel to have someone else in trouble instead of herself.

The wide boulevard went under the arch of an ancient Roman aqueduct, and soon they were passing modern apartment buildings in a pleasant residential section. Gradually, the road narrowed and the traffic increased as they followed the cobblestones and sharp turns of old city streets. It was growing too dark to see very much, but against a sky of fading gold and amethyst were silhouetted the rounded shapes of mosques and the many needlelike points of minarets.

Mrs. Byrne drove anxiously now, with considerable worry about other cars. "The way Turks drive!" she said in annoyance as a car cut recklessly across her path. "Believe me, I can hardly wait to get back to the U.S.A. and stay there for good!"

"Turkey's not so bad when you get used to it," Ken said.

Mrs. Byrne was concentrating on the snarl of traffic as the road descended toward a strip of water. "The Golden Horn," she said, "for whatever it's worth to you." She sounded as though it wasn't worth very much to her.

Vicki remembered Aunt May drawing the lines of a map. Now the lines were suddenly alive. They were boats on a dark strip of water and lights climbing the hills ahead and behind. They were a bridge crossing from old Istanbul into the new, where office buildings and banks and hotels rose on every hand.

Vicki thought of a question she wanted to ask. "Dad wrote that there was a castle near where you live," she said. "Is it a real castle from the old days?"

"Castle?" Mrs. Byrne repeated doubtfully. "Oh, you must mean Rumeli Hisar. It's a fortress on the Bosporus. We'll drive around the base of it this evening, but it will be too dark to see anything. You'll have a good view from your room in the morning. It's real enough, and more than five hundred years old, I think."

The drive out toward the suburb of Bebek, near which Mrs. Byrne lived, was a long one. In the back seat, Vicki began to feel a bit sleepy, lulled by the swish of passing traffic and the dancing of lights on the fine new highway. She drowsed until Mrs. Byrne spoke again.

"Here's our hill," she said, and turned up a narrow winding road that climbed upward from the water.

Vicki roused herself and sat up, but there were only a few scattered lights to be seen out there in the darkness. As they made a final turn, the shape of a large house with lighted windows loomed beside the road. Mrs. Byrne turned the car into a driveway and drew up before a modern garage.

"Welcome to our pasha's palace," she announced. "Jump out, Ken, and help with the bags. Your father isn't home yet, Vicki—the Volkswagen isn't here."

So again the meeting with her father was to be postponed for a while. Vicki got out of the car and stood looking up at the house. It was a large, two-story structure, oblong and boxlike in shape, with a gently slanting roof. The part that extended toward the Bosporus was well lighted, while the uphill section stood dark and a little forbidding. It was odd to see a house cut in half by its low lights. A wide veranda ran along the entire back at the second floor level, and she could make out long windows beyond the veranda, closed and shuttered tight. To her right, across the driveway, she could glimpse a dark garden, with trees rustling softly in a breeze that blew uphill from the water.

"Was he a three horsetail pasha?" she asked sleepily.

Ken said, "Wha-at?" and Mrs. Byrne laughed.

"I know what she means, Ken. I suspect that he was a rather unimportant pasha, since the house was not built on the water's edge and is far from being a real palace. Come along inside, Vicki, Ken will bring your bags."

The breeze against Vicki's face had the cool touch of early May, with enough sharpness to waken her and clear away some of the cobwebby unreality. She followed Mrs. Byrne through a rear door and into a narrow hall. This in turn opened into a much grander hall where wide stairs mounted to a landing and turned upward to the floor above. The lower hall was a great room in itself—a room with a stone-paved floor and a tiled fountain in the center. A tiger cat ran across their path, and Mrs. Byrne said, "Shoo!" and clapped her hands at it.

"Sometimes I think Turkey has more cats than anything else," she said.

Except for a bench or two there was no furniture in the stone-floored room, and it seemed a cold place tonight, though it might be pleasant during a hot Turkish summer. The polished stairs were rugless and electric sconces lighted the way up.

"You'll find the house more Victorian than Turkish," Mrs. Byrne said. "It's somewhat less than a hundred years old, and it was build when wealthy Turks thought it fashionable to copy the styles of Western Europe. Though there are Turkish touches too. Tell her about the haremlik, Ken, and take her up to her room, will you? I must go and see what's happening to dinner."

A pretty Turkish maid came out to speak to Mrs. Byrne. She wore a printed house dress and white apron. Her hair was hidden beneath a white square of cloth tied about her head. Mrs. Byrne waved a casual hand at Vicki, who had started upstairs after Ken.

"Adria knows you're arriving. Do run in and see her

before you come downstairs. Ken will show you her room."

Then she was gone, and Vicki was climbing the wide, dark stairs beneath a lofty ceiling that seemed to vanish high overhead.

# 3

# Adria

The stairs opened into a large salon above, furnished with comfortable modern sofas and tables, chairs, and lamps, though all were set about sparsely because of the space they had to fill. Here and there a few richly colored Oriental rugs were scattered. A wide hall ran the entire length of the house, taking in one side of the salon and terminating at the far end before huge closed doors.

"Mom keeps that part shut off," Ken said. "The house is too big for us to use all of it. In the beginning she rented rooms and small apartments to Americans living out here. But now that Dad is being transferred home in the fall, it's not worth bothering with. So we occupy the selamlik part and take in a few friends. Dad's doing some work around Ankara now, so there's no one here but you and your father. Oh—and Adria, of course. That's the haremlik beyond those big doors."

"I don't know what you mean by haremlik and selamlik," Vicki said as she turned her back on the doors and went through the salon to the front end of the house.

"The selamlik—this part—was the men's living quarters," Ken said. "The haremlik was for the women. All the old Turkish houses were built like that, even to having separate gardens and entrances. Adria says the Turkish ladies are still in there rustling around in their silks and bangles, ready to pop a veil over their faces if a man shows up who doesn't belong to their family. But what can you expect from Adria? Watch out for her or you'll start being goofy too."

28

The presence of Turkish ladies seemed an odd notion, but then almost everything seemed odd at the moment and Vicki made no comment. She didn't mean to judge Adria until she saw her for herself.

Ken pushed open a door and turned a switch. Overhead a lovely chandelier came into glowing life. Prisms and crystal teardrops split the light into miniature rainbows and illumined the room with bright radiance.

"You must rate," Ken said. "This is one of the best rooms in the house. I don't know why such a fuss was made to put you here. Especially when—" he broke off and grinned as he set down her bags. "Especially when you're in disgrace."

Vicki stared at him in dismay, and he winked like a conspirator.

"Never mind. I don't always get good marks in school either. At least you'll have a few extra weeks of vacation this way."

So her father had told, Vicki thought miserably. She did not like Kenneth Byrne very much, she decided. Wishing he would go away, she put her feelings into one of her darkest scowls.

"O.K.," he said. "I get it. You needn't bite me. We'll be having dinner soon, so you'd better wash up. The bathroom is just beyond the stairs at the start of the long hall. Adria's room is right across from it. If you want to stop in to see her, I wish you luck."

He left the door open when he went out and Vicki made no move to close it. Compared with her bedroom at home, this room seemed enormous. The ceiling was high and distant, with a diamond shaped design in its wood paneling. The windows were very tall, with dark-figured green draperies shrouding them. She went to the nearest one and parted the curtains to peer out, but it was too dark to see very much. She could make out the veranda running past, with arches and slender pillars framing the outside edge. The night seemed dark and cold, and she shut it away hastily and turned back to the brilliance of her room.

The feeling that she had been holding off all this time

came close now and threatened to engulf her in misery. It was a loneliness that had started back home when she had said good-by to her mother, and it had been growing stronger ever since. In it there was a longing for her own little room with the whispery willow tree outside, a longing for her mother, even for Aunt May, who loved her and was her own family. Here there seemed to be no one she belonged to, or who belonged to her.

She took off her hat and coat and laid them on the bed as if she were a visitor who would be leaving soon. She made no move to open her bags, and she did not look at herself in the shadowy mirror over the big old-fashioned dressing table that was all curlicues and carving.

There was no friendly welcome here, and she wanted to escape the room as quickly as possible. Gathering up the towel and soap that had been laid out for her, she went down the echoing hallway to the bathroom. With a sidelong glance she noted Adria's door. It stood ajar and a faint sound emerged from it—a sort of whispered chant that she could not understand.

Washing made her feel a little better. She hadn't realized how sticky and grimy she was from the trip. A bit of tugging with a comb helped to get her hair in order, and when she had taken her towel back to her room, she was ready for the next step.

The open door of Adria's room seemed to beckon her. So many strange things had been said about Adria March that she was curious to see for herself what this girl was like. Besides, she had no desire to run downstairs immediately and find herself again in Kenneth Byrne's company. Adria might be the lesser of two evils, and she needn't stay more than a moment—time enough to say "hello."

Nevertheless, she approached the open doorway uncertainly. The odd, murmuring whisper still sounded from the room. Should she knock? she wondered. Was someone in there with Adria? Gathering up her courage, she stepped across the sill and stood on the threshold of Adria's room.

It was a smaller room than her own, and there were fewer windows, though the ceiling was as remote and high, the furniture as big and old-fashioned. A shaded lamp burned on a bureau and a modern reading lamp had been attached to the head of the bed, pouring its light down upon a slight, fair-haired figure sitting up against huge pillows.

Adria March was the prettiest thing Vicki had ever seen. She was like one of those advertisements in a fashion magazine—all perfection and not quite real. Her hair, falling gracefully over her shoulders, caught the golden glint of the lamp over her head. A wide blue band of ribbon held it back from a forehead unpuckered and smooth. At the moment Adria's eyes were tightly closed, and her lips were moving, murmuring words over and over, but so softly that Vicki could not make them out. The girl had drawn her knees up beneath the covers, and her two fists were clenched upon them—the only sign of tension in evidence.

Vicki hesitated uneasily, not knowing whether to advance another step into the room, or turn and go quietly away. She shifted her weight, trying to make up her mind, and a board creaked beneath her feet. The girl in the huge bed stopped whispering and opened her eyes. They were not blue eyes, as Vicki had expected, but sea gray, rainy day gray, and they stared at Vicki as though they could see through her and behind her and all around her. It was such a strange look that Vicki blinked the lids over her own brown eyes several times.

Someone had to speak, and since the girl in the bed did not, Vicki made an effort.

"Mrs. Byrne said I should stop in and say hello. But if you're saying your prayers or—or something—I'll just—"

The yellow-gold head moved quickly from side to side. "Don't go away. I know who you are. May your coming be pleasant. That's what we say in Turkey. I wasn't praying. I was telling myself who I am."

Vicki frowned in bewilderment, and the girl in the bed laughed out loud. It was a light, silvery sound, and Vicki remembered what Aunt May had said about a flute.

"Don't frown at me," said Adria. "Haven't you ever tried to tell yourself who you are? I do it often. There are three ways. *I* am Adria. I *am* Adria. I am *Adria.* But I can't be sure which one does it best, so I try them all, over and over. Sometimes it helps a great deal. Sometimes it surprises me, and I start wondering who Adria really is."

It was difficult to find anything to say in response to such a surprising statement. As if a person could lose track of who she was. But Vicki couldn't stand there saying nothing again, and with an effort she wiped the frown from her forehead and said the first ordinary thing that came into her head.

"I'm sorry about your cold."

Adria's smile made her look prettier than ever, but it was not exactly a happy smile.

"It's not a cold," she said. "Cousin Janet—that's Mrs. Byrne, who is a very distant relative—worries about her responsibility to me. She thinks I ought to catch cold after what happened yesterday, so she put me to bed. I'm glad you've come. I was getting bored. Did they tell you what I did?"

Vicki shook her head. "Ken mentioned something about the rain."

Adria laughed again. "It wasn't the rain that mattered. At least not the wetness of it. Getting wet was an accident. It was the sounds I wanted to hear. Do you ever listen to sounds, Victoria?"

"Everyone calls me Vicki," Vicki said lamely. She had never in her life felt so bewildered by another girl her own age as she felt with this strange, rather beautiful young person in the bed.

"I'll call you Victoria," Adria said. "It's fun to roll out all those syllables—they have a wonderful sound." She slipped out of bed and ran barefoot across to a window, pushed the shutters wide, and leaned her pajama-clad elbows upon the sill. "Come here and listen," she said.

Drawn in spite of her bewilderment, Vicki went to the window. There was no veranda here. The window looked out toward the winding road that Mrs. Byrne had followed up the hill. At first she heard only the wind in the trees, but then her ears caught other sounds—frogs croaking in the darkness, the distant barking of a dog, a mournful drawn-out whistle nearer at hand.

"That's a boat whistle, isn't it?" she asked. "It sounds like our river boats at home."

The girl beside her nodded. "The Bosporus is down there. I can't see it from this window the way you can from yours, but there are always boat sounds to be heard."

From somewhere in the garden a bird song suddenly trilled, and Adria put a hand on Vicki's arm to hold her silent till the last sweet note had lost itself in velvet darkness.

"A nightingale," Adria said softly, and Vicki felt a queer little prickle go up the back of her neck. A nightingale! She had actually heard a nightingale.

"My father used to say that hearing was as important as seeing because of all it could make us feel. Do you know about my father? Look—I'll show you."

The slender, graceful figure in blue pajamas, bright hair dancing as she moved, flew across the room and turned a light switch. A chandelier, not quite so elaborate as the one in Vicki's room, sprang to glowing life, and Adria moved toward a wall of the room. Except for one thing, the wall was completely bare, and all furniture had been moved away from it. In the center, plainly occupying a place of honor, hung a framed painting. There was no glass covering it to reflect light and blur the picture. Adria waved a hand at it proudly.

"My father was an artist. A very good artist. I think he might have been great and famous someday, if he hadn't been there in Switzerland when the avalanche came down."

She spoke so calmly that Vicki stole a startled look at her, wondering if she herself could have spoken without tears of an accident that had taken the lives of both her parents only a short while before. Adria's face was ashine with love and pride, but at the moment she wasn't grieving.

"Listen to it," she said. "Listen to all the sounds he painted into that picture."

Vicki stared at the rainy forest scene as if she had been hypnotized. A storm was sweeping through the trees, streaming through tortured, outflung branches, and she could imagine the roar of the wind, the staccato beat of rain, the wet slap of dead leaves hurled against a tree trunk. Adria was right. She had never thought of "listening" to a picture, but the man who had painted this one had been thinking of sounds. The sensation was strange—something she had never experienced before.

With one of her lightning movements, Adria switched off the chandelier and returned to her bed, pulling up the covers.

"Do you believe in spells?" she asked.

Keeping up with Adria was a little like flying in a plane, Vicki thought. Everything went too fast, and she felt left behind, with much that was in the past not yet understood or finished with.

"Of course I don't believe in spells," she said. "At least I haven't since I was about six."

Adria watched her soberly for a moment. "No, I suppose you wouldn't. But don't forget—this is Turkey. Very strange things can happen here. I had my fortune told by a gypsy—a gypsy who is a friend of mine." She held her hand palm up toward Vicki. "She told me there was a spell in my hand, but she wouldn't tell me what it meant."

The sound of a Chinese gong boomed musically through the house, and Adria flicked her fingers at Vicki. "That's the signal for dinner, Victoria. You'd better run. I'll see you tomorrow."

As quickly as that, Vicki found herself shut out. It was as though a door had closed in her face. Adria had shut her eyes, and her lips were moving once more in a faint whispery sound.

More than a little dazed, Vicki went into the hall-salon. It looked vast and bare in spite of the furniture scattered around. A sound of voices and the odor of appetizing cooking drifted up the stairs. She dreaded going down there, but she couldn't very well retreat to her room, and in spite of all she had eaten on the plane she found herself growing hungry.

As she walked slowly toward the stairs, she closed her eyes and murmured to herself: "I am Vicki. I am Victoria. I *am* Vicki." But the words were not at all reassuring. She had the queer feeling that she had lost touch with Vicki Stewart and that some stranger inhabited her body and put queer thoughts into her mind. Did she believe in spells? Goodness, how silly could she get! She gave herself a good hard shake, and suddenly she was Vicki again. Quite cross and resentful, too, because her father had not bothered to come to the airport to meet her. A fine welcome she'd had, after coming all those thousands of miles across oceans and continents clear to the edge of Asia!

She started down the bare stairway, her steps thumping firmly, disagreeably on the creaking steps, and made the turn at the landing. A man stood at the foot of the stairs, looking up at her, a man with a thick brown beard trimmed and shaped as neatly as a gardener might shape a hedge. White teeth flashed in the dark beard as he smiled at her, and she realized that the bearded man was her father.

"Hello, Vicki," he said. "I'm awfully sorry I couldn't meet you."

With the new beard, he didn't look like Dad, and she went down the stairs uncertainly, shyly. When she reached the second step from the bottom, he did not wait, but put his hands on her arms and swung her down to his level, enveloping her in a hug. She clung to him, her arms tightly about him, sudden tears in her eyes. This *felt* like Dad. If she didn't look at the beard, she could believe it was her father.

"How are you, honey?" he said. "And how was Mother when you left?"

She told him haltingly, and he kept an arm about her shoulders as they walked toward the dining room. The disagreeable mingling of depression and gloom lifted a little. At least he wasn't going to be stern right away and lecture about her failure in school.

They walked into the dining room together, and she found it a big room, furnished with large old-fashioned pieces that probably belonged to the house. Mrs. Byrne and Kenneth were waiting.

The four of them were lost at the long table, even though they gathered at one end of it. As the Turkish girl brought in the food, Mrs. Byrne kept up a running conversation and Dad joined in quietly, though infrequently. Now that he was across a table from her, Vicki found the beard once more got in the way. He seemed like a stranger—someone she had never seen before.

Ken gave most of his attention to eating, though once he cocked an eyebrow at Vicki and asked under his breath if she had seen Adria. She nodded and let it go at that. She had not sorted out her reactions to Adria as yet, and she didn't want to talk about her to Ken.

Dad must have caught the mention of Adria's name, for he asked Mrs. Byrne about her.

"I hope she's feeling better," he said. "Has there been any trouble today?"

Ken's mother sighed. "No more than usual. The child bewilders me completely. Her head is stuffed with the most utter rubbish. I can't think how her parents must have raised her, since she has such queer ideas."

"I always liked Gerald March," Dad said. "He was something of a genius, and geniuses are seldom like other people. I suspect that Adria is as wildly imaginative as he was—which doesn't always make for practical everyday living. I suppose there's nothing much to do about her except be patient. She'll grow up eventually."

Vicki caught the barest flick of a glance in her direction and found herself speaking a little defiantly.

"Adria showed me a picture her father painted. That forest-in-a-storm picture that's hung on her wall. She showed me how to listen to it."

Ken rolled his eyes. "I know! As if anybody could paint sounds!"

Dad chuckled. "I don't know but what that's an interesting idea."

Again he flicked a look in Vicki's direction—as if he wondered what she was thinking. She kept her eyes on her plate and said nothing more. It was safer just to eat.

Fortunately, the food was delicious. There were little rounds of lamb and vegetables that had been cooked on skewers and served on pilaf. Kebab, Mrs. Byrne said, was a popular Turkish dish, and she had thought Vicki might enjoy it for dinner. Vicki did and finished up every bite while her father began to speak with enthusiasm about the man he had interviewed today. An authority, very difficult to reach, he said, who had put him on the trail of some most unusual mosaics and tiles in a little known mosque.

Vicki paid little attention. Now that she had eaten, she was tired and sleepy, and she was beginning to feel cross again. Unpleasant thoughts were turning about in her mind, and she made no effort to push them away. Because of some old tiles, Dad had been too busy to come to the airport to meet his only daughter. In a way it would have been more reassuring if he had scolded her right away about her failure in school. At least, that would have shown that he was thinking of her. Tiles on the walls of a mosque were more important to him than she was. By the time she had finished the cheese pastry and fruit that were served for dessert, Vicki had stirred up all her smouldering resentment against her father.

When Mrs. Byrne said, "Let's have our coffee in the sitting room," and moved back from the table, Vicki slipped gladly from her chair.

"You children may be excused," Mrs. Byrne said. "Ken, since this is Vicki's first evening here, perhaps you could—"

There was a dawning in Ken's eyes of reluctance to do whatever his mother was about to ask, so Vicki yawned widely.

"I'm sleepy," she said.

Mrs. Byrne nodded. "Of course, you are. It will take a few days to adjust to the time change after your long trip. Would you like to see my Turkish sitting room before you go up to bed?"

"A good idea," Dad said, but Vicki did not look at him.

She wasn't interested in sitting rooms at this moment, but there was nothing to do but follow the others to a room that opened off the stone-paved hall. It was long and rather narrow, with arched windows along one side.

"It's more Turkish in character than most of the house," Mrs. Byrne said. "I've shopped in the bazaars and furnished it as authentically as I could."

Under the windows were low, soft divans with colorful striped covers and bright cushions. Little tables, inlaid with mother-of-pearl or small pieces of decorative wood, were placed here and there. Several framed pictures hung on the walls. If you could call them pictures. As nearly as Vicki could make out, they seemed to represent the queer curves and dots of old Turkish writing.

Dad noted the direction of her gaze and explained. "Since the religion of the country forbade any reproduction of human or animal figures, old Turkish art concerned itself with abstract design such as you find in tile work and architecture. The Turks were interested in this sort of decorative calligraphy, or writing. Those framed examples are probably quotations from the Koran, the book that is to Moslems what our Bible is to us. They often used this sort of thing instead of pictures on the walls. These seem to be fine specimens, Mrs. Byrne."

He sounded terribly like a professor lecturing, Vicki thought crossly. But Mrs. Byrne seemed pleased by his approval. Ken's mother was a lot older than her own mother, Vicki decided critically, and too big. It pleased her to find as many things wrong as possible.

Mrs. Byrne moved to a corner cabinet of glass in which was arranged an assortment of small figures and animals, bowls and tiny vases. They were of carved ivory and porcelain, cinnabar, ebony, and other exotic materials, Mrs. Byrne explained.

For the first time Vicki's interest came to life, and Ken's mother, noting it, went on enthusiastically.

"I've been collecting these things for years. Some of them come from Africa and China and Japan."

She forgot that Vicki was sleepy and opened the glass doors to take out a small golden object encrusted with tiny jewels that twinkled in the light.

"I found this in the bazaar a few days ago. It's quite

nice handwork." She held it out for Mr. Stewart and Vicki to see. Vicki looked at the jewel-set miniature that was a little like the curving horn of an animal.

"Very nice," Dad said, taking it onto his palm. "It's a good piece. You must have done some bargaining for it."

"I did. But when the dealer was sure I was going to walk out empty-handed, he came down almost to my offer." She turned it over, indicating a clasp on the back. "It's meant to be worn as a pin, but I wanted it for my collection. The stones are only semiprecious, of course."

"It's appropriate," Dad said, "to have a golden horn from Istanbul. Go up to Sultan Selim Mosque sometime and look down at the water. By moonlight, or even in bright sunlight, the Golden Horn looks rather like this."

Mrs. Byrne returned the brooch to its place beside a wooden rhinoceros from Cape Town. Then she turned again to Vicki. "I have one rule about this collection. No one touches these things but me. I even dust them myself. But if you're interested, I'll be happy to show you the pieces sometime. Now I know you want to get to bed. Is there anything you'd like before you go upstairs? Anything you need?"

Vicki swallowed a yawn and said there was nothing.

Her father gave her shoulder a pat. "Run along to bed, honey, before you fall asleep on your feet."

Vicki said good night collectively to everyone and made no effort to go to her father for a hug and kiss. It was a relief to run upstairs alone and find her way to the door of her big corner room. Now she was prepared to stay in it and shut out the world. It was a strange room, but the world outside was even stranger and more unwelcoming.

She opened her bags sleepily, undressed, and got into her pajamas. The real unpacking would have to wait until tomorrow—though she knew Aunt Laura would never approve. When she had run down the hall to the bathroom to wash and brush her teeth, she was ready for bed. She turned off the flood of light from the chandelier but left a small lamp burning on the bed table. Then, somewhat doubtfully, she approached the high, old-fashioned bed. It was the biggest bed she had ever seen, with a headboard that rose up the wall in dark carving that culminated in a fat cupid at the top. There were two huge pillows and a great depth of covers and quilts. It was a bed made for a giant, and she felt quite inadequate to fill it. Not even Adria's bed was as big as this.

Before she climbed into it, she would open a window, she decided. She chose one that was not on the veranda side and figured out how to work the catch so that the glass doors swung inward. As she was examining the fastening on the outer shutters, she heard a faint scratching sound behind her and whirled about, startled.

She was alone in the room and though she glanced uneasily toward shadowy corners, nothing moved. Then, quite softly, the scratching came again. Of course—it was at the door.

She went to it and put her hand on the big brass doorknob. "Who's there?" she asked. It couldn't be Dad. He would give the door a good bold knock, not scratch on it secretly.

"Let me in! Let me in quickly!" said Adria's voice.

The door wasn't locked, and Vicki opened it at the awkward catch near the floor. In an instant the slim figure in blue pajamas bounded into the room and shoved the door shut behind her, as though someone were in pursuit.

# 4

# Pattern of the Horn

Vicki stared at her visitor in surprise. She was not sure she welcomed her at this moment when she was ready for bed and so sleepy.

The blue band of ribbon was gone from Adria's fair hair, and she had braided it into two long, thick pigtails for sleeping. The braids hung forward over each shoulder, and now and then Adria picked one up and tickled her nose with a wispy end.

"I thought you might be lonesome tonight," she said. "I was when I came to this house for the first time. Now that I'm used to it, I like it. It's so queer and spooky, and there's so much history all around. If only Cousin Janet—"

She did not finish her thought about Cousin Janet. Instead, she drew a hand from behind her back and held it out to Vicki.

"I brought you a present."

Dangling from her fingers was a string of blue beads a little longer than choker size. They were cool and smooth to Vicki's fingers as she took them into her hands.

"Put them under your pillow tonight," Adria said. "They're to keep away the evil eye."

Then, without waiting for an answer, she took them back, ran across the room, and thrust them beneath a huge pillow on the bed. Next she went to the shutters Vicki had been about to open and unlatched them, pushed them back, and fastened them with hooks against the wall.

"There! You have a beautiful view. That band of dark down there is the Bosporus. And you can see the lights of Anatolia on the other side. That's Asian Turkey. We're in Europe. I have a friend at school who lives in a village over there."

Vicki followed the quick, pointing finger with her eyes and saw the lights of a boat moving between the two shores. To her right something huge and black blocked out a whole portion of the water, so that she had to look to either side to find the Bosporus.

"The walls and towers down there belong to Rumeli Hisar," Adria said. "Our European side is called Rumeli, and Hisar means fortress. There's a fortress across on the Asian side too—Anadolu Hisar. But it's not as big, and this is the one I like best. Leyla stayed inside the walls all night once, and no one knew. I'd like to do that myself if I had the chance."

"Who is Leyla?" Vicki asked, waking up a little in spite of herself.

Adria held out her hand with the palm up as she had done before. "She's my gypsy friend. The one who told my fortune. The gypsies will be coming again soon. They bring down lavender from the hills and sell it in town every spring. Leyla will know about what has happened to me. She'll find me. Then I'll get her to tell my fortune again and show me what I must do to make it come true."

Vicki knew what Ken would say to all this. But though Adria was strange, she made things interesting, and she kept the loneliness away. For the moment at least.

Adria shivered and turned back to the room. "It's cold tonight. I'm going to bed. You'd better go to bed too, instead of leaning out the window."

This was hardly fair, since it was Adria who had opened the shutters and pointed out the view, but before Vicki could answer, Adria made one of her unexpected right-about turns and asked a point-blank question.

"Is it true, Victoria, that you failed in your work at school so you won't be promoted with your class?"

Vicki had endured all she could. Quite suddenly she

disliked Adria and Ken and Mrs. Byrne—and her father most of all.

"That's nobody's business! Nobody's business at all!" she cried. "Why don't you go away and leave me alone?"

Adria closed her fingers about each of her blond braids and tugged at them as if she needed leverage to move her head.

"My, but you get mad fast," she said calmly. "There's no use playing ostrich, you know. Even if you hide your head in a hole, we can see the rest of you. We all know you're a problem to your family. Cousin Janet has been worried about your coming because she already has what she calls 'a major problem' with me. Of course, I'm glad you've come for that very reason. Now she won't concentrate on me so much."

"Oh, go away," Vicki repeated crossly. She turned her back on Adria, kicked off her slippers, and crawled into the vast bed. When she had wormed her way down between cold sheets, she opened one eye and looked out at the room. Adria was still there, watching her.

"When you were little and your mother was home, did she used to come and tuck you in at night?" Adria asked.

"Of course," Vicki said gruffly. She reached out a hand and turned off the lamp beside her bed, leaving Adria in the dark, to go or stay as she pleased.

Adria chose to go. She opened the door, and a flood of light from the hall streamed in. "My mother used to tuck me in too," she said and went away, drawing the door very softly shut behind her.

Now what had she meant by bringing that up? Vicki wondered. But she did not think about Adria for long. How easily tears came when she was alone in the dark. There was a queer aching deep inside her. An aching that nothing seemed to help. She wasn't sure what it was that she ached for. She simply hurt and wept silently into the big pillow under her cheek.

In spite of the hurting, however, she was tired, and was just dozing off when she heard her father's voice, speaking to her through the door.

"Are you asleep, Vicki?"

At once she knew what the aching came from. Adria had reminded her. It was because Dad hadn't thought of coming upstairs to say good night to her. Yet now that he was here, a queer thing happened. The knot of resentment and contrariness, which had begun to wind up inside her, rolled into a solid ball of resistance. She closed her eyes tightly and did not answer.

When the door opened, the glow of light from the hall pressed against her closed lids, but she lay very still and tried to breathe deeply as if she were asleep. After a moment of waiting, he went away and when he had gone she pounded her pillow fiercely with one fist.

"Go back to your old tiles and your history!" she whispered, and pounded the pillow again.

She was glad he had gone without coming in. She did not want to speak to him at all. He would remember about school and lecture her—which she could not bear. It was bad enough that he had betrayed her to all these people. Why couldn't he have given her a chance to hold her head up and start out fresh with new friends? After all, that was why she had run away to Turkey. But because he had told, all her problems were here ahead of her, and everyone knew. Her father was a stranger with a beard anyway. She didn't really know him or want to.

Her pounding fist had found the blue beads Adria had thrust under her pillow, and she drew them out and ran them through her fingers. Protection from the evil eye! She'd had enough of Adria too. With a quick gesture she flung the beads out into the dark room and heard them strike something and clatter to the floor.

Now she wasn't even sleepy any more. Why couldn't people leave her alone, instead of waking her up when all she needed was a good rest? She turned and tossed in the expanse of the big, strange bed and wished for her narrow bunk at home. She tried lying on her back, lying on her stomach, and lying on each side. Nothing helped.

Somewhere outside in the darkness, a voice began to sing—the first note a long, drawn-out "Ay"—melancholy and strange. The voice was a woman's, very clear and beautiful, but the song was like nothing she had ever heard before. It was mournful, heartbreaking—a few minor notes up and down a limited scale. Not music as Vicki knew it, but something Oriental and sad. Surely a song of loss and sacrifice and sorrow. Listening to it, Vicki began to feel that her own hurt and anger was being drawn out of her to center in a song that spoke for all who sorrowed anywhere. She wondered if Adria heard it too. Adria, whose grief was far more serious than her own.

Sleep came easily and gently now, and Victoria Stewart did not waken again through all the long night.

Indeed, she did not waken until well into the morning. When she opened her eyes, the eastern sun was pouring through the tall oblong of the open window, and the night shadows had vanished from the big room. Overhead the chandelier caught the sunlight, enmeshing it cheerfully in its many prisms. Vicki yawned and stretched and rolled out of bed.

When she looked into the hall, she found a rosy-cheeked maid bustling around the salon, dusting and polishing. The girl smiled at her and said what was probably "good morning" in Turkish. She made a gesture of eating and pointed to the stairs. Apparently Vicki could still have breakfast, and she discovered that she was ravenously hungry. She returned the girl's smile before closing the door and looked at her watch. It was ten o'clock. High time to be up and exploring.

When she was ready to go downstairs, she felt much better than she had the night before. Nothing seemed quite so strange, and she no longer felt completely lonely and unloved and betrayed. It was true that her father— but she put the thought of him quickly from her mind. She did not want to remember pretending to be asleep when he had come upstairs last night.

In the dining room she had scrambled eggs, hot toast, and milk, plus a delicious jam that was like nothing she had ever tasted before.

Mrs. Byrne looked in while she was eating and though she seemed distracted and hurried, she made nothing of Vicki's oversleeping. Probably she was used to that with Ken.

"Good morning," she said. "Have a good rest? You look fresh and bright. I wonder if you can manage for yourself this morning while I drive to market? Your father and Ken have gone, of course, but the servants are here, so you won't be alone."

"I'll be fine," Vicki said, feeling so cheerful that she surprised herself.

"Perhaps you can make your own bed when you've finished breakfast," Mrs. Byrne went on. "Then you can look around the house as much as you like. Except for occupied bedrooms and my Turkish sitting room, which is private. You can go out in the garden too. But don't wander away outside until you know the neighborhood."

Vicki nodded, her mouth full of toast and jam.

Mrs. Byrne smiled as though in relief that Vicki had offered no objections. "That's Turkish rose petal jam you're eating," she said. "Ken likes it too." She started for the door, hesitated, and turned back. "I forgot to mention Adria. She's to stay in bed another day. Perhaps you'll keep an eye on her while I'm gone. You can visit if you like, but she's not to get up. See you later."

She waved her hand and went quickly away, leaving Vicki to sip her milk and think over the fact that *she* had been left in charge of Adria. That, at least, was a task she didn't welcome. She had every intention of avoiding Adria's room. The more she thought about Adria, in broad daylight, the more she felt inclined to agree with Ken. Adria was strange and a little creepy. Keeping an eye on her would be a little like keeping an eye on a bit of quicksilver or a shooting star.

When she had eaten all she wanted, she went upstairs, dutifully made her bed—a rather difficult task, considering its size—and then began to unpack and hang up her dresses in a big wooden wardrobe that served for a closet. Once or twice she went to the window and looked out at the tremendous view.

The pasha's house was set well up a steep hill, much higher than the line of fortress walls and towers below that made up Rumeli Hisar. She could see the high gray stone wall of the fortress, crenelated along the top in cas-

tle fashion. At each corner of this rear wall rose a large
round tower, much like a castle in itself. But the wall was
too high to see what lay beyond, and she turned her attention to the wide, blue Bosporus, where numerous ships
and small boats were visible this morning.

The sight of the fortress had reminded her of something
and when she tired of watching the view, she took out a
big folder she had packed into the bottom of her suitcase.
The bed made a good place to lay out her castle collection.
In spite of Aunt Laura's objections, she had brought the
pictures with her. So far, she had forty-two views of castles
from all over the world. There were several from Scotland—Dunvegan Castle on the Isle of Skye, and Edin-
burgh Castle—among them. And of course Windsor Castle from England. Nijii Castle was in Kyoto, Japan, and
there were castles from the Rhine country and Austria,
and the Castle of Chillon in Switzerland. A picture of
Rumeli Hisar would make an important addition, and it
would have the further advantage of being the first real
castle she had ever seen in person. She must remember to
ask about getting inside it later. Adria had spoken of her
gypsy friend spending a night there, but that wasn't
Vicki's ambition.

As she moved about the room, her foot struck the blue
beads Adria had given her last night. She picked them up
and examined them by daylight. They were a lovely blue
in color, each one about as large as the end joint of her
little finger. They seemed to be made of opaque colored
glass, and sunlight glanced off them and made them shine.
In one respect, they were disappointing. They could not
be worn because there was no clasp. The strand was
joined together by a long, decorative bead through which
the green cord on which they were strung was joined. It
was knotted in a finial bead at the end. The string wasn't
long enough to slip over her head, and she wondered what
the beads were used for. Besides keeping off the evil eye,
she thought, making a little face as she remembered
Adria's nonsense.

Before long she'd had enough of unpacking and being
indoors. She opened a French window and went out on

the veranda. The tawny cat she had seen last night lay asleep in the sun. At her step, it opened its eyes and stared at her with the slitted yellow gaze of a tiger. It was the look of an owner regarding a trespasser, and Vicki left the cat alone.

Through high carved arches that framed the long balcony she could look down onto the garage and driveway and toward part of what seemed to be an enormous garden. Beyond the stone wall around the property, glimpsed here and there through foliage, she could see occasional white houses, some with red tiled roofs, dotting the slopes of a cleft between hills that ran down toward the Bosporus. Above, the hills were gently rounded, thick with pine woods and dark strands of cypress. There was room to spread out in this country along the Bosporus with none of the crowding that existed in Istanbul.

Most of what had once been a pasha's garden was out of sight around the house, and from that direction she heard thin, high strains of music, as if someone was blowing into an instrument. She decided to go downstairs and investigate the sounds.

Tiptoeing past the door of Adria's room, not wanting to be heard and summoned inside, she hurried downstairs. Following the lower hallway along the route she had taken last night, she found her way outdoors. The morning was warm and beautiful. She hardly needed the sweater she had flung about her shoulders. She could no longer hear the piping of music, but a frog orchestra had taken over and was tuning up noisily.

The garden was so large that much of it was no longer tended and grew pleasantly wild, so that before long she was almost lost in shrubbery and weedy growth. Idly she followed a path that led past a tiled fountain where water played. Beside it grew a tree completely afroth with purplish-pink blossoms. She wandered past a wisteria arbor, dripping lavender flowers, and through a thick grove that seemed like a bit of forest.

Here she turned and stood looking back at the long box of a house in the bright morning light. Beyond the unused portion of the veranda the haremlik was shut behind the lattices of many shutters, empty now of all the bustle of color and life that must once have existed there.

Having no idea from what direction the piping sounds of music had come, she was content to wander without purpose. Along the far boundary of the garden stretched a stone wall higher than her head, but before she reached it, a sunny little glen caught her eye.

Small fig trees with twisted branches arched above it, and low shrubbery shut it in, though the grass was green inside where a patch of sunlight fell through. It was almost like a secret cave, half hidden by trees and brush, though open to the sky. As she stopped to enter the little clearing, a voice stopped her.

"Don't go in there!" it called sharply.

Vicki turned to find Adria behind her, as if she had sprung out of the ground. There were two things to be considered about this daytime Adria. She was supposed to be in bed with a cold. Instead, she was up and dressed in a white frock that flounced with stiff crinoline under-petticoats. Her hair was loose and neatly combed, and this time a rose-colored band of velvet held it back. Her slippers were white and spotless. Altogether Adria, at eleven o'clock in the morning, was not in bed but dressed up as if for a very special party.

Vicki said the only thing that occurred to her. "Mrs. Byrne said you were to stay in bed today."

Adria laughed. "Mrs. Byrne is an old silly. I haven't any cold. But I might as well take advantage of staying home from school today."

"Are you going to a party?" Vicki asked.

"Party? Oh, you mean because of my dress? No, but I'm expecting company, and I feel partyish. So why shouldn't I dress up?"

Vicki gestured toward the sunny glen within the twisted barrier of trees. "Why don't you want me to go in there?"

"It's forbidden," Adria said solemnly. Then she laughed again at Vicki's expression. "It's forbidden because I forbid it. If you go in there now, you'll spoil everything. I'm waiting for the light to be right, and I don't want anyone to move the branches around. Wait a little while, and I'll show you."

Vicki regarded her curiously. What made Adria so different from any girl she had ever known? she wondered. So annoying, yet so fascinating.

"Have you always lived in Turkey?" she asked.

Adria had turned to look for something in the grass behind her. She found it, pounced, and tucked it away beside a stone, answering Vicki over her shoulder.

"I was born in Ankara when my father was teaching painting there. But we moved to Istanbul a few years ago, and I like it better here. Mustafa Kemal—he was the first president, you know—built up Ankara as the capitol, so that it's modern and beautiful, but I like old Istanbul best. Would you like me to play for you?"

She had picked up a long wooden instrument that Vicki recognized, since she had seen recorders at home. Adria waited for no invitation but flounced out her skirts and sat down on a flat-topped boulder. She put the recorder to her lips and began to blow. With a few bars Vicki recognized the tune. It was "Little Buttercup" from *H.M.S. Pinafore,* and she smiled in recognition. Adria played it quite well, and Vicki sat down on the grass to listen. Since Adria was apparently not going to mention the matter she had brought up last night about school, Vicki was glad to have someone for company.

"That was fine," she said when Adria blew the last note and laid the recorder down on the grass beside her.

"The music club girls from the Orta Okul are going to give some excerpts from *Pinafore,* and I'm in the orchestra," she said.

"Orta Okul?" Vicki repeated.

"Yes—that's our prep school. 'Orta' means middle. It's like a secondary school in the States."

School was not Vicki's favorite subject, and she asked no further questions.

"I was playing my recorder when I got rained on and was supposed to have caught my death of cold. I was here in the garden practicing when it started to rain. The rain sounds were wonderful, and I was trying to imitate them when Mrs. Byrne started shouting for me. I was so interested that I didn't notice how badly soaked I was."

She broke off and dropped to her hands and knees, creeping toward the sunlit glen without much care for her white dress. In the bright light of morning Vicki saw that her eyes looked, not sea gray, as they had last night, but sea green, and they were alight with a strange eagerness. When she reached the patch of sunlight she studied it thoughtfully for a moment and then looked around at Vicki.

"I do believe I'm right," she whispered. "I believe the shape is what I thought it was. Come here and look. Tell me what you see."

Puzzled, Vicki knelt beside Adria and stared through the tangle of shrubbery to the space of sunlight that marked the ground within the glen.

"What do you mean?" she said. "There's a spot of sunlight on the ground and shadow all around. So what?"

"Sh-ssh!" Adria said, as if the sun patch might hear her and vanish. "What is it shaped like. Tell me!"

Vicki regarded the spot critically. "Well, it's curved sort of live—maybe like a yellow banana."

"Banana!" Adria cried in disgust. "Isn't it like a curved horn? A golden horn, perhaps? Or perhaps like—"

She broke off and ran back to the rock where she had left her recorder and reached into a hollow of earth beside it. With something in her hand, she returned to kneel beside Vicki.

"Like this!" she finished and opened her fingers.

In surprise and dismay Vicki stared at the small jeweled object Adria held out to her. It was the little golden horn from Mrs. Byrne's precious collection.

# 5

# Over the Wall

Vicki was shocked into silence. She stared at the pin in growing horror.

Adria seemed not to notice her dismay. "Don't you think the shape of that sunny patch in there is a little like the curve of this horn? Like the curve of Istanbul's Golden Horn?"

"It looks like a banana to me," Vicki said flatly. "And you'd better put that back right away before Mrs. Byrne finds out that it's missing."

"Oh, I'll put it back," Adria said airily. "I've only borrowed it for a little while."

"But why? What if a sun patch does look like a horn or a banana? What's the difference?"

Adria's sea-green eyes had a dreamy look. "I don't know exactly. But I know there's something I must find. And when I find it—no, I won't tell you. You don't know anything about Turkey. And you don't believe in spells."

Several possible remarks went through Vicki's mind. Such as "Of course I don't," or "Don't be silly!" but she spoke none of them. There was something about Adria's faraway look that kept her from making fun. For an instant it seemed as though Adria's eyes had turned gray again and were brimming with tears.

Then she jumped up with a whirl of white skirts and ran back to her rock where she tucked the jeweled pin into its hollow of grass and picked up the recorder. This time she paid no attention to Vicki when she put it to her lips, and the notes that floated out upon the air were mel-

ancholy and haunting. As she played, Vicki recognized
the same sorrowful tune she had heard a woman singing
off on the hillside last night.

She was about to say so, but Adria looked at her in-
tently and blinked her eyes without faltering in her
playing. It was, Vicki recognized, a signal for silence. A
strange thing was happening. From behind the high stone
wall that marked the edge of the garden, came a voice
singing as it had sung the night before, blending in with
the mournful tune of the recorder.

Adria played through to the last wailing note, and the
human voice followed. Then she jumped to her feet and
ran toward the wall.

"It's Leyla!" she cried. "I knew the gypsies had come
when I heard her singing last night. I knew she'd be here
today."

Following more slowly, Vicki heard someone scram-
bling up the wall from the other side. A moment later a
girl's head appeared above it—a head with thick, tousled
black hair, through which strings of colored beads had
been threaded. The brown-skinned, animated face that
looked down at them was very pretty as the girl smiled a
greeting for Adria. She called out something Vicki did not
understand and pulled herself up so that she could sit on
top of the wall.

She was probably eighteen or nineteen, Vicki decided.
She wore a rumpled white blouse with full, loose sleeves
and a wide, red cotton skirt flowered with splashes of yellow. About her neck hung numerous strands of bright
beads, and gold hoops were fastened in her pierced earlobes. From beyond the wall a child's voice called, and
she reached a hand down to help someone else up the
wall. A moment later the scrawny figure of a little girl appeared beside her. The child was about seven and seemed
to be dressed in odds and ends of clothing given her by
people who were older and larger. Her small, impish face
was grimy and her hair, with its narrow bandeau of blue
beads, looked as though it had not lately seen a comb.

"You've come, Leyla! You've found me!" Adria cried.
"I knew you would."

"We find O.K.," said the older girl and looked question-ingly at Vicki.

Adria drew her forward. "This is my friend Victoria. Victoria, this is Leyla and her sister Cemile."

" 'Allo," said Leyla and prodded the child beside her. "You tell 'allo, Cemile."

Cemile tried to hide behind her mat of hair but man-aged an echo of her sister's greeting. Vicki said, "Hello," and waited with interest to see what would happen next. The thought crossed her mind that Mrs. Byrne might not approve of gypsies, but she dismissed it at once.

"I invite you to come in," Adria said, waving a hospit-able hand toward the garden.

The gypsy girl did not hesitate. She took the hand of her little sister, and they jumped down into the garden. Then she touched Adria's fair head with a light caress. Vicki sensed that it was as if the gypsy had told Adria that she knew of her parents' death and that she grieved for her out of her own heart. Adria gave her a misty smile and murmured something in Turkish. Then she gestured toward the sunny glen.

"Leyla, I've found something. Come and see."

Leyla took her time. She looked around the overgrown garden and stared at the big silver-gray house that had once belonged to a pasha. Only the tiled roof and a few upstairs windows were visible from this place, the rest hid-den by the lush growth of the garden.

"Is good," she said and moved her hands in a wide, graceful arc. "Like a palace."

"My Cousin Janet rents it," Adria said. "I liked our lit-tle house in Bebek better."

In response to Adria's directions, Leyla dropped to her knees and peered into the clearing. She seemed to under-stand at once what Adria meant, for she turned her head this way and that, even looking at the sunny space upside down through the crook of one arm. Her eyes were adance with laughter and gaiety now.

"No—is not the same," she said at length. "Is not the golden horn."

"Then maybe this is it?" Adria said. She picked up the

little pin she had hidden near the rock and held it out to Leyla. Cemile, who had been dancing around the garden in delight, came to see, and everyone stared at the jeweled horn on Adria's palm.

Leyla touched it respectfully with her finger. "Very pretty. But no, I do not think—can be—but I do not think."

Adria sighed. "Then how am I to find the sign? How am I to know?"

"You can know," Leyla said gravely. "When is right, you can know."

Adria seemed momentarily disappointed, but she turned her attention to other matters.

"Did you bring them?" she asked. "Did you bring the things for the fortunetelling?"

Leyla's laugh reminded Vicki of her singing. It was melodic, but with a melancholy note in it, as if the weight of many troubles lay upon gypsy shoulders even when a gypsy laughed out loud.

"I bring," she said and dipped into a voluminous pocket in her flowered skirt.

In a moment she had brought out a goatskin pouch closed with a drawstring. As she opened it, Cemile came to stand beside her sister, watching. Her bright, dark eyes were as eager as Leyla's, but it was Adria she watched, rather than the ritual. In fact, Vicki realized, the child was mimicking Adria, standing as she did, moving when she moved. Leyla saw and shook her head reprovingly, but Adria only laughed.

"Cemile wants to be an American," Adria said. "She can copy me if she likes."

"Cemile is gypsy," said her sister in a tone that settled matters, and Cemile did no more copying.

In uneasy fascination, Vicki watched Leyla smooth a place in the earth and then pour out a handful of glass beads and flat dried beans from the pouch. These she threw upon the earth, scattering them. Frowning, she squatted before the array and studied it with great concentration. Apparently she did not like what she saw, for she gathered everything up and cast the beans and beads again. Then in silence, without explaining anything, she picked them up, put them away in the pouch, and drew the string tight.

Adria watched in disappointment. "Was it such a bad fortune that you can't tell me about it?"

The gypsy girl shrugged and would not say. Moving unexpectedly toward Vicki, she caught her right hand and turned it palm up, bending the fingers back and forth as if to test their flexibility. Startled and more uneasy than ever, Vicki was tempted to snatch her hand away, but she did not quite dare. With a slender, slightly dirty finger, Leyla traced the lines in her palm, her big, dark eyes alive with excitement.

"Is sign here also! Sing of Golden Horn!"

Adria moved closer, and as she held out her own right palm, Vicki bent her head to follow the pointing gypsy finger and saw that the same curving double lines that crossed her own palm seemed to mark Adria's hand as well. They were not very long or clear lines, but they were there.

"What does she mean?" Vicki asked. "What's she talking about?"

Adria spoke a few quick words of Turkish to the gypsy, but Leyla only smiled and tossed her head. Her rapid answer was spoken in the same language. Adria interpreted as solemnly as though she believed every word.

"She says our fortunes are tied together. The beads and the beans she cast show that bad things are going to happen to us. But when we find the Golden Horn, everything will be fine. If we do not find it"—she snapped her fingers—"disaster. But this she does not understand. She doesn't know whom it threatens." Adria moved closer to Vicki as if for reassurance. "Victoria, I think—I'm afraid."

Vicki did not like the sound of any of this.

"So it is some sort of golden horn we must find," Adria went on. "Leyla says you're in great trouble too, and there will be worse to come. But she doesn't know, or at least she won't tell me any clues as to where to look for the thing that will help us."

Vicki was glad when Leyla let her hand go. She believed none of this, and she liked it less and less. How could Leyla know about what trouble she was in? Or whether it would get better or worse? Though it was an easy guess that Vicki's particular troubles were likely to get a lot worse.

A trilling whistle like a bird call sounded from beyond the stone wall, and Adria forgot the fortunetelling.

"It's your uncle, isn't it, Leyla? Come up the wall with us, Victoria."

Leyla called to Cemile, but the child had disappeared, so she climbed the wall nimbly without waiting. She reached down and pulled Adria to the top beside her, then held out a hand to Vicki. Curious to see Leyla's uncle and know what lay beyond the wall, Vicki took her hand, found toe holds in the rough stone, and went easily up beside the other two.

In the grass beyond the wall a surprising sight awaited her. A large brown bear lay dozing upon the ground. Beside the bear stood a swarthy-skinned, black-mustached man in shabby black trousers, gray shirt, and a loose black vest. In one hand he held the end of a double chain attached to the bear's muzzle and to its red leather collar. At the sight of the three girls looking down at him from the wall, the gypsy flashed a broad smile, made them a ceremonious bow, and with a flourish caught up a tambourine from the ground. When he tugged at the bear's chain, the animal lumbered to its feet. Its master thumped the tambourine and chanted a song, while the bear waved its paws vaguely, moving from side to side on its hind legs in a dance without gaiety.

Vicki felt sorry for the bear. His coat looked rough and scraggly, and he did not seem to be enjoying his work. The others appeared to take the whole thing for granted, and when Adria untied a few coins from a knot in her handkerchief and dropped them into the man's palm, Vicki looked away from the bear.

Up here on the wall, she could see something of the countryside beyond the house grounds. The hill road curved past the garden and ran out of sight around a

clump of trees higher up. Across the road was another
stone wall—a very long one—marking private property.
Close at hand beside the road, grazed a donkey with
panier baskets across its back, and she wondered if Leyla
and Cemile traveled by this means.

Layla called for her sister again, and when the child
came into view, she cried out in anger. Vicki and Adria
looked down at once to see that Cemile, her eyes mis-
chievously alight, was dancing toward them through the
garden. Her odd assortment of clothes made her look like
a tiny scarecrow, but her slender arms were completely
filled with flowers. She had broken off a branch from the
pink flowering tree, she had pulled down a spray of
wisteria, and a mass of yellow tulips finished off her huge
bouquet.

Leyla cried out in Turkish and dropped into the garden
from the wall. Before Cemile could move, she had boxed
the child's ears and shaken her, scolding all the while. Cemile began to cry, screwing up her small face and wailing
out loud. Now it was Adria's turn to be indignant. She
scrambled down the wall and ran to put her arms about
Cemile and hold her away from her sister.

"Don't punish her!" Adria cried. "It doesn't matter if
she picked the flowers. Let her have them. There're plenty
more where they came from."

Cemile smiled through her tears and leaned close to
Adria, looking up at her gratefully.

"I beat him good," Leyla said, mixing up her pronouns
in her anger over Cemile's violation of hospitality.

"No you won't," said Adria, and Vicki admired her for
taking the gypsy child's part. Cemile looked thin and not
very strong, as though the hard life of a wanderer might
not agree with her.

Vicki was about to climb down from the wall herself,
when a new voice made itself heard.

"Adria? Vicki? Girls, where are you?"

Oh, dear, Vicki thought, Leyla's prophecy of trouble
was going to come true even more quickly than expected.
Through the trees she could glimpse Mrs. Byrne's blue
dress as she approached this outlying part of the garden.

"Here we are," Adria answered. "We're over by the wall, Cousin Janet." To Vicki's surprise, she sounded perfectly calm and undisturbed.

When Mrs. Byrne reached them, she was far from calm. Her attention focused first on Adria. "What are you doing out here when you're supposed to be in bed? An all dressed up like that as well?"

At the first sound of her voice, Cemile had scampered behind a tree without dropping her burden of flowers. But Leyla stayed where she was, and Mrs. Byrne gestured toward her.

"What is that gypsy doing here?" she demanded of Adria.

"Leyla is my friend," Adria said calmly. "Every spring the gypsies come down from the hills to sell lavender. My mother always bought from Leyla, and she hopes you will too."

"I might buy if she comes to the door properly," Mrs. Byrne said. "But not if she sneaks into the gardens behind my back. Tell her to go around to the door."

"She came into the garden because I invited her," Adria said with dignity. "And she understands what you are saying. She speaks a little English."

Leyla called to her sister sharply, and Cemile sidled out from her hiding place. With one look at Mrs. Byrne's shocked expression, she dropped her armful of flowers, scuttled for the wall, and went up it like some small terrified animal. Watching her, Mrs. Byrne saw Vicki, still balanced on the broad top of the wall. She stared for a moment and then turned despairingly toward the scattered flowers.

"This is too much," she said. "Come into the house at once, girls."

With a long sigh over the flowers, she walked away through the trees without waiting to see if she was obeyed. Before Cemile left her perch to follow her sister, she stuck out her tongue and made a face at Mrs. Byrne's retreating back.

Adria knelt and picked up the tulips. "They'll be all

right in water," she said. "But the wisteria and the flowers from the Judas tree are crushed."

Vicki could only marvel at her calm. "I expect we're in for it now. We'd better go back to the house right away."

They walked through the garden together, but Adria did not hurry.

"She's furious, isn't she?" Adria said, sounding pleased. "But I won't let anyone be rude to Leyla. My father liked gypsies. He used to paint them sometimes. Once he did a very good sketch of Leyla and gave it to her. These Romany people are my friends."

Mrs. Byrne had paused near the rear steps to wait for them, and she heard Adria's words. "Gypsies are not to be trusted," she told her. "You can never tell what a gypsy will do. I don't want them on my property, Adria. Please understand that. The child was too young to know better about the flowers, but one of you could have stopped her. I must say I'm disappointed in you, Vicki. I'd hoped you would keep Adria entertained and in bed. She's home from school today for the sake of her health, you know."

Vicki couldn't see how she could have done anything to keep Adria in bed. Especially since the other girl was already up and out of the house ahead of her. But she made no attempt to explain these things to Mrs. Byrne. Adria's Cousin Janet was too annoyed to be argued with.

"I'll go look at the gypsies' lavender and get rid of them," Mrs. Byrne said as they went into the house. "But, Adria, please don't ask them onto our property again. I don't want to quarrel with anything your father and mother did, but you are living with me now."

"Yes, Cousin Janet," Adria said more meekly than Vicki would have expected. "May I stay up if I change my dress? I don't really have a cold."

Mrs. Byrne paused in the hallway of the house to put a hand on Adria's forehead. "If you're sure you're all right, I suppose you can go back to school this afternoon. Do try to keep out of trouble until then. Both of you."

She left them near the foot of the stairs, and Adria grinned at Vicki. "My, but you look mad. I'll give these tulips to Fatma to put in water. Then let's go up to your room, and I'll tell you about Leyla and Cemile. They're only half gypsy. It's a very romantic story."

Vicki was not sure whether she was more indignant with Mrs. Byrne for her injustice, or for Adria for getting her involved in this escapade. She did know that she wanted no more trouble so decidedly not of her own making. When Adria returned from the kitchen, she put her main worry into words.

"Did you bring the pin back from the garden?" she asked.

Adria tossed her head, and the soft blond hair floated about her shoulders at the movement. "Of course not. Do you think I want to be caught? I hid it in the hollow beside that big rock. I'll return it when it's safe."

"Remember that I had nothing to do with your taking that pin," Vicki said.

Adria surprised her with a sudden, winning smile. "I'll take the blame if anything goes wrong. Come along to your room, and I'll tell you about Leyla."

Somewhat reluctantly, Vicki followed her upstairs. She could only hope that Mrs. Byrne would not decide to show the new piece in her collection to someone before Adria put it back.

# 6

# The Trouble Begins

Sheltered as it was by closed shutters, Vicki's big bedroom was almost as cool as it had been the night before. But Adria flew about, opening the veranda doors, pushing the shutters ajar, flinging wide the window from which the Bosporus could be seen.

"I love sunlight! I love to be warm!" she cried. "This is a beautiful room. I wish it were mine. It was good of your dad to give it up so that you could have it."

Vicki stared in surprise. "You mean this was my father's room before I came?"

"Didn't Cousin Janet tell you? He thought the view might make up for the way you'd feel when you first arrived. He said he didn't mind taking a smaller room—he could work anywhere. Not that there's what you'd call a small room in the entire house. Hey—what's this?"

Adria, moving about in her quicksilver way, had reached the bed where Vicki had left the collection of castle pictures spread out in rows across the coverlet. She was not sure she wanted Adria to see the pictures, but it was already too late.

"These are wonderful," Adria said and picked up first one and then another. "What fun you must have with them! This castle with the stairway going up into a tower, for instance. The picture is so clear you can almost climb the steps and look into the room above."

Vicki was pleased. She had never known exactly why she loved pictures of castles. But unlike Aunt Laura, Adria seemed to need no explanation. She accepted it as a good idea and walked right into the pictures as if they themselves were as real as Vicki tried to imagine.

"There are some wonderful old castles in Turkey," Adria said. "You must see Rumeli Hisar. But now let's talk about gypsies."

She curled herself up in the room's one big armchair, and Vicki put some of the pictures aside and sat cross-legged on the bed, listening as Adria told her Leyla's story.

"Her mother was a Turkish girl. A gorgio, as the Romany people call nongypsies. The family lives in Istanbul. Leyla's grandfather is a retired Army officer. He was terribly upset when his daughter fell in love with a gypsy and ran away with him. Leyla and Cemile were born among gypsies and lived that way until their gypsy father died a few years ago. Then their mother returned to her family in Istanbul and brought the two girls with her. She and Leyla went to work as maids in an American household in Bebek, and they took little Cemile with them, as maids with children do when they go to work in Turkey. That's how it happens that she and Leyla speak a little English."

"Then why did they go back to being gypsies?"

"Their mother died too, and Leyla couldn't wait to join the gypsy tribe again. Her grandparents wanted both girls to stay with them, but Leyla is truly a gypsy. She doesn't want any other life. So she took Cemile and went back to gypsy ways. My mother and father knew her when she worked as a maid for friends of ours. After she became a gypsy again, she used to drop in to see us whenever they came near Istanbul. That's why I knew she would go to the place where we used to live and ask questions about us. I knew she would find me. If she hadn't, I'd have left word sometime with her gorgio family in Istanbul. I know where they live. I visited them once with my mother and father."

The faraway look was in Adria's eyes again, as though she was remembering happier times.

"Isn't it strange," Vicki said, "that your mother and mine were good friends when they were our age? Did you know that?"

Adria nodded. "Your father told me. That's one reason I was anxious for you to come."

Vicki felt unaccountably touched. It was hard to be annoyed with Adria for long.

"Why don't you explain about Leyla to Mrs. Byrne?" She asked gently. "Tell her what you've told me."

"She wouldn't understand," Adria said. "All she thinks about is getting home to America. She doesn't like Turkey or any of the other places she has lived. My father used to say that there are some Americans who never fit into life in a foreign country. They want everything to be the way it was at home. Of course, it never is, so they're critical and dissatisfied. Mrs. Byrne is counting the days until she can leave—about six months from now."

"What about you?" Vicki asked. "Will you be going home with the Byrnes?"

The flash in Adria's eyes was like sudden green lightning. "Turkey is my home. I don't know anything about America, except from books and from what people say. Maybe I'm like Leyla is in wanting to be a gypsy. I want to stay here. But I don't have any other relatives except Uncle Hinton, whom I can't stand. He's my mother's older brother, but he was never very nice to us. Besides, he travels all the time and doesn't live in one place."

Adria left her chair and crossed the big room to the bed. Before Vicki knew what she intended, Adria caught her right hand and turned it palm up as Leyla had done. Beside it she set her own smaller hand and stared earnestly at the two palms.

"We'll find it together," Adria said. "Whether you like it or not, we're tied together in the search for a golden horn."

Vicki drew her hand away uncomfortably. "What do you think would happen if you found whatever it is?"

"I don't know," Adria said. "Last year when Leyla came to see us in Bebek, she pointed out the mark in my hand. She said the dreadful things would stop happening when I found what I must search for. How could she know what was going to happen when it hadn't even started then—unless she has second sight? They say some gypsies do have it, you know. Now you're in it too, and you've got to help me look for it."

Vicki had heard enough of such notions for one day. "I'm not going to look for something when I don't know where to start, or what it is, and when I don't believe in it in the first place." She slid off the bed to end matters. "I think I'll go wash up for lunch. I'm dirty from climbing that wall."

Adria stared at her for a moment, her eyes unreadable. Then she dashed for the door ahead of Vicki. Beyond the big salon the door of Adria's room banged shut, and Vicki knew that the other girl was offended. She couldn't help that. Adria's problems were real enough, but she couldn't work them out with gypsy spells. The sooner she came to her senses the better.

At lunch Mrs. Byrne still seemed annoyed, and Adria was lost in her own silence. So Vicki ate more or less in silence too, answering Mrs. Byrne when she was spoken to but making no remarks of her own. As before, the food was delicious, and she enjoyed the white Turkish cheese and red tomatoes. Conversation did not seem necessary.

Right after lunch, Adria went down to the waterfront to take a bus the short distance to school. Mrs. Byrne said she was going upstairs for a nap, and Vicki found herself with a long, empty afternoon stretching ahead of her. Mrs. Byrne had said she might follow the road for a little way, either up or down the hill—she couldn't get lost on it. So when she was alone, Vicki started out in the bright spring sunshine, choosing the downhill course.

The road was narrow and paved in asphalt where it dipped steeply toward the walls and towers of the fortress below. As she followed it, Vicki thought of her strange morning and of all the disturbing things that had happened. She thought of Adria and the troubles she seemed to be creating for herself, and she came to a conclusion. Having made up her mind, she felt better. There was one thing she might do to help, whether Adria approved of it or not. Now she could take real pleasure in her walk of exploration.

The road changed to cobblestones and separated in a Y

where it ran behind the fortress. She chose the right-hand
turn and followed it toward the water. The castle walls
and great round towers were impressive close up, but she
did not want to attempt a castle visit now.

The waterfront road was busy with traffic. Diesel engine
buses and trucks, smoking blackly, ran noisily up and
down the narrow way. Beyond, the waters of the Bosporus
lapped only a little way below the edge of the land. Fishing boats with curved prows, their interiors brightly painted, were drawn to the shore, and great fishing nets dyed
green and brown and bright blue were spread out to dry.
Across the water on the Anatolia side a white palace
shone in the sun, and there were domed mosques here and
there with their adjacent minarets. Up the hills behind the
villages on the other side the pink blossoms of Judas trees
spread delicate color.

She did not want to walk too far this first time, and before long she turned uphill again toward home. As she
climbed, she began to make up a letter to her mother in
her mind. She would write it today and send it off airmail.

She would tell her mother about Adria, whose mother
had been her friend when she was a young girl. And
about the gypsies, Leyla and Cemile. But not about how
angry Mrs. Byrne had been, or about the little sword pin
Adria had taken from her Cousin Janet's collection. There
would be no need to mention that because it would no
longer be a problem. She was going to do something about
it herself. And right away.

The house was quiet when she let herself in the front
gate. Walking quietly around to follow the paths of the
garden, she passed the fountain, the flowering Judas tree,
the wisteria arbor, and soon she was again in the wild part
of the old garden. Here under the plane trees, it was
shady and cool, and she found her way to the little glen
where a streak of sunlight had so interested Adria that
morning. Now the shadows had changed, and the sun was
gone from the encircled patch of grass.

Without difficulty, she found the rock where Adria had
sat, and put her hand into the hollow beside it. There was
nothing there. She got down on her hands and knees and

carefully separated the stalks of grass and weeds, searching through them with her fingers. But though she searched persistently all the way around the rock, she found no jeweled pin.

When she was sure that her search had been thorough, she sat down on the rock to think. This was a foolish place to hide such a tiny object. In her hurry, Adria could have let it slip out of her fingers anywhere, so that it might never come to light again. A careless foot might press it into the earth. Adria's recorder lay in plain sight on the ground where she had forgotten it, but no amount of looking brought the pin to light.

It was possible, of course, that Adria had slipped out here alone, retrieved the pin, and put it back in its place. She could move like the wind, or as secretly as a little ghost, so she could have managed this sleight of hand right under Mrs. Byrne's nose. Surely that was what must have happened. But Vicki knew she would not feel comfortable until she made sure.

She picked up the recorder and went back toward the house. Everything was quiet, sleeping. As before, all the veranda windows in the closed-off harem part of the house were shut and had a deserted look about them. How queer it was to live in a house where numerous rooms were closed off completely, so that no one ever went into them! Sometime she would like to see that part of the house. But now now. There was something else she must do.

Quietly she let herself in and tiptoed through the narrow hall to the place where it opened out into the great, cool lower hall at the foot of the stairs. It was off this that Mrs. Byrne's Turkish sitting room opened. There were several doors, however, and the first one she tried was the wrong door. The next was right, and she pulled it open upon shuttered darkness. A little nervously she sought for a light switch and turned on the overhead chandelier. She would not go in, of course. She would stand here in the doorway and look. If Adria had returned the horn, then she ought to see it quickly enough.

But the problem was more difficult than she had expected. Mrs. Byrne's collection was rich in so many objects of varied size. Now that she could view the big cabinet in the corner, she was no longer sure exactly which place the pin had occupied. There was a little space between an ivory elephant and a satsuma bowl. Was that where it had been? Or had it been on the shelf above, where small lacquer boxes showed a gap? As far as Vicki could tell, no gleaming golden horn lay among the other objects.

Still, she could not be sure from here, since it wasn't very large, and she wanted to be positive. She went into the room, still on tiptoe, breathing quickly now and moving with a sense of imminent danger. She did not know the ways of this household and at any moment she might be discovered. Yet the objects on the shelves drew her. The glass reflected electric light confusingly, so she opened the cabinet door and stood looking carefully at the collection.

How fascinating these things were! A tiny Japanese lady carved in ivory walked pigeon-toed, with an ivory umbrella held over her head. Vicki put her hands behind her back, lest she be tempted to touch, to pick up. She wasn't here to admire the collection but to locate one special object.

The voice behind her came without warning. In a way she was not surprised. Discovery seemed part of the pattern of bad luck that dogged her steps.

"What are you doing here, Vicki?" Mrs. Byrne asked. Her tone was quiet, but that fact was not reassuring. Vicki sensed that Mrs. Byrne was holding herself in check.

She turned about, trying desperately to think of something to say. She could feel her face burning in a betrayal of guilt—when there was nothing to betray.

"Well?" Mrs. Byrne said curtly.

"I—I was just l-l-looking," Vicki stammered. "Your collection is so interesting."

"I believe I offered to show it to you myself," Mrs. Byrne said. "And I'm sure I told you that this room is private."

Vicki said nothing at all. When Mrs. Byrne walked to the cabinet, straightened a small bowl, and closed the door, she held her breath. At any moment she might look toward the place where the horn should be and discover that it was missing.

"I can't wait to get these things home," Mrs. Byrne said. "I only hope I can manage without having anything broken or stolen."

Vicki found herself wondering how Ken's mother could show such enthusiasm about collecting the art work of foreign countries without liking the countries or the people in them. It was a relief when she stopped touching and straightening and led the way out of the room, closing the door behind her. Her evidence of displeasure was clear.

"It won't be long now before everyone comes home from school. Do you suppose you can amuse yourself without getting into trouble until that time?" she asked.

Vicki nodded silently and went upstairs to her room. She felt cross again and unjustly treated, but at the same time almost limp with relief because nothing more serious had happened. If Mrs. Byrne only knew it, *she* was the one who had been trying to protect the collection. But she could not explain without betraying Adria, and she had no wish to do that. As she went upstairs, she decided that Adria must have brought the pin from the garden and hidden it in her own room, to wait for an opportune moment for returning it. She could only hope again that Adria would put it back before Mrs. Byrne found out it was gone.

In her bedroom Vicki sat down at a small table to write the letter to her mother. The words would not come as easily now as they had earlier in her mind, and before long she gave up. She read for a while, but her thoughts kept wandering from her book.

Somehow the next hour dragged by and when Ken came home from school she heard him and went out to the veranda to call down to him. He gave her a careless wave of his hand and walked toward a small shedlike addition that had been built at one side of the garage. Ken's company would be better than no one at all, Vicki decided, and ran downstairs to find him.

"Is it all right if I come in?" she asked at the door of the shed.

Ken turned on an electric bulb that hung from the ceiling and as he looked around at her, she saw in surprise the angry expression on his face.

"Were you out here in my workshop today?" he demanded.

Vicki felt that she'd had about enough of the Byrnes' suspicions.

"Of course I haven't been!" she snapped. "I didn't know you had a workshop, and I wouldn't have come into it if I had."

Ken ran a hand through his carroty hair and stared at her. His scowl was as black as Vicki's own. Tools had been taken down from the wall rack and heaped in a jumble on the bench. A screwdriver and hammer had been dropped on the floor. A glass bottle holding screws had been tipped over and a box of nuts and bolts turned upside down.

"How did it happen?" Vicki gasped. She couldn't blame Ken for being mad, and her own indignation died a little.

"How do you suppose?" Ken said grimly. "Somebody came out here and jumbled everything about. And I know who it was."

Vicki had an uncomfortable feeling that she knew too, but she didn't want him to speak Adria's name. She leaned past him and reached for the bottle that had held the screws.

"I'll help you straighten up," she said. "Do you want these back in the bottle?"

Ken nodded grumpily, but he accepted her help, and they went to work together. At first neither said anything, but as the workbench began to look more shipshape, Ken cheered up a little and began to talk. From a high shelf he took down the model plane he was working on and showed it to Vicki with justifiable pride. It was a model of an old-fashioned biplane.

"At least she didn't hurt this," he said. "If she had, I'd—I'd—"

To stop him from finishing the threat, Vicki plunged into an account of how Leyla and Cemile had come over the wall that morning, telling him about the dancing bear but leaving out his mother's annoyance.

There was no knowing whether Ken was interested or not, but he let her talk without interruption until she mentioned fortunetelling.

"I hope you don't believe that stuff," he said. "Adria's nutty when it comes to spells and fortunes. But why she should come out here and mess up my things, I wouldn't know."

The accusation was out in the open between them now. It could be concealed no longer.

"Perhaps you teased her," Vicki said. "Perhaps she was trying to get even with you for something."

"If I teased you, would you play a trick like this?" Ken asked.

Vicki considered the question. "No, maybe I wouldn't. But I might try to get even with you in some other way. At least she didn't damage anything, did she?"

"That doesn't mean she won't next time," Ken said.

Vicki put the question that was troubling her most. "Are you going to tell your mother?"

"I don't know." Ken shrugged. "I ought to tell her." But he had stopped looking angry, and he threw Vicki a curious glance. "You don't want me to tell her, do you?"

"I suppose not," Vicki said doubtfully. "Adria's had so much trouble. Losing her parents in that terrible accident. Having to come into a strange home where nobody really loves her."

Ken gave his careful attention to a gluing operation on his model. Then he set the plane down and wiped his fingers.

"You can be sorry for a person up to a point," he said. "But after that some of the trouble he makes for himself is his own fault. It's that way with Adria. What does she expect from a trick like this except more trouble? How *could* anyone love her?"

"What if it wasn't Adria?" Vicki asked on sudden inspiration.

Ken laughed. "Who else is there to play such tricks? The servants are all friends of mine. And no one would come in from outside, mess up my workshop, and run away. Don't worry—it was Adria, all right. I never thought it was you."

Grateful for that, at least, Vicki wandered to the door of the workshop and stood looking up at the house, trying to figure out the puzzle of such behavior. Her eyes rested upon the haremlik section where shuttered windows faded into shadow as the sun dipped toward western hills on this side of the Bosporus. How fanciful the carving was in the weathered shutters! There seemed to be little perforations in the latticework, so that someone standing in those rooms might look out at the world, without being seen. Of course that was what the latticework had been intended for—to shelter cloistered Turkish women.

As she studied the shutters beyond the many-arched veranda, the queer feeling came over her that someone was watching her. It wasn't possible to see the eyes she felt were fixed upon her, but the feeling of being watched was so intense that she turned to Ken.

"Does anyone ever go into those harem rooms?" she asked.

Ken must have caught the uneasy note in her voice, for he came to stand beside her and look up at the house. For an instant it seemed to Vicki that a shadow moved behind the shutters. Then all was quiet, and the sense of being watched was gone. With a grin, Ken went back to his model.

"Who would go into a lot of empty old rooms?" he said. "There's nothing there. You're seeing Adria's Turkish ghosts who walk around the harem at night, and probably come down here when they've nothing else to do and play tricks with nuts and bolts and screwdrivers."

He was teasing her good-naturedly, and she knew he would not believe it if she told him someone up there had been watching them. Probably it was Adria, though why she should go into that unoccupied part of the house and spy through the harem shutters, Vicki didn't know. But then—who could ever guess what Adria would do next?"

Back at his work, Ken was busy again, forgetful of Vicki's presence. There was nothing else for her to do here. Idly she wandered into the garden. Perhaps she would have another look for the pin, though it was getting a little dusky for that.

Rounding the turn of a path, she came upon the small fountain. Beside it, studying the pattern of its yellow and blue tiles, stood a man with a small, neatly trimmed beard. At her step he looked around and smiled.

"Hello, Vicki. I was wondering where you were. Come and walk with me in this Turkish garden."

A quick rush of affection for her father swept through her. All else around her was strange, but Dad was hers, and the beard did not matter.

# 7

# Behind Latticed Blinds

They walked along companionably. Her father was not treating her like a four-year-old now but telling her about the tiles of the fountain, pointing out a crooked fig tree with its gray bark and large leaves, showing her a bed of bright-yellow Turkish tulips, the petals edged delicately with red.

"Most people don't realize," he said, "that the tulips of Holland came originally from Turkey. Turks love flowers. In the old days, this must have been a very beautiful garden."

She glanced up at him and thought how distinguished-looking he was, even though she couldn't get used to the beard.

"Thank you for my room," she said. "Adria told me it was yours, and you moved out so I could have it. It's a lovely room."

He looked pleased. "Aunt May wrote me about how hard this trip was for you. Leaving Mother, leaving your friends and summer plans to come out to a strange country must have been difficult. I thought the room might make up for a little of what you were losing. I'll be glad if it does."

Nothing could make up for what she had lost, but she didn't mean to tell him that.

"I hear there was some sort of gypsy escapade today," he went on, sounding more amused than disturbed.

So Mrs. Byrne had already been talking. If only she had not told him about catching her in the sitting room looking at the collection, Vicki thought. She didn't mind talking about the gypsies, and she gave him an account of what had happened, even to Cemile's picking of the flowers and Leyla's fortunetelling. She had never found her father so easy to talk to, or felt so grown up and accepted in his company.

He seemed sympathetic about Cemile. She was probably accustomed to gathering blossoms that grew wild in the fertile parts of Turkey she traveled through, he said. But he thought Leyla's fortunetelling a joke.

"I wouldn't set too much stock in what a gypsy girl tells you. It's true that there are strange things in this world of ours—things we can't always explain with our present knowledge. Perhaps they'll seem logical enough when we know more about such matters. However, I think Leyla enjoys being dramatic and taking Adria in with this fortunetelling. Adria's father knew Turkish gypsies rather well, and I've heard him talk about them a bit. Fortunetelling is done mainly by the old crones of a tribe, and a good deal of it is fakery, of course. Leyla is probably imitating her elders and playing a role she enjoys. But don't take her seriously."

"Would she make up something about disaster?" Vicki asked doubtfully.

"Why not? That would be the most dramatic touch of all. And if she was pinned down, she could always say it was trouble in the past that was indicated, not in the future."

Vicki found his words reassuring, though she wondered if it would do any good to repeat them to Adria.

"What about the marks Leyla said were alike—in Adria's hand and mine?" she questioned.

"Probably every hand has such marks," he said. "Show me what you mean."

There was still light enough in the sky for her to trace the curved double lines in her palm, and her father considered them seriously. Then he held out his own hand and pointed to lines that were similar—but not exactly the same. Not the identical markings that seemed to exist on Adria's palm and hers.

They walked on again, and Vicki's thoughts returned to Adria's troubles. "You knew Adria's parents, didn't you?"

"Yes, I did. Though they went off on their unfortunate trip through Europe shortly after I came here at Gerald's suggestion. I liked them both a lot. Gerald March was an unusual and gifted man, and his wife a charming, sensitive woman. I suspect that Adria is a lot like her—or will be when she gets over this very difficult time she is going through. I hope you'll be friends with her, help her all you can."

Vicki offered no comment. This might be a harder assignment than Dad dreamed. There were too many uncomfortable things that were adding up against Adria. Things that promised trouble: The taking of Mrs. Byrne's pin—even though she only meant to borrow it; the mischief in Ken's workshop; the spying from shuttered windows in an empty part of the house. These were things she could not explain to her father.

"I tell you what," he said as they turned back to the fountain that made a central focus in the garden. "Saturday morning I'm going to drive in to Istanbul to look at some tiles in a mosque. How would you like to go with me? We'll ask Adria too, and then she can take you through the Covered Bazaars and introduce you to one of the most interesting cities in the world."

"I'd love that!" Vicki told him warmly. It would be a good thing to get Adria away from Mrs. Byrne and Ken, get her mind off gypsies and fortunetelling.

Dad gestured to a marble bench near the fountain. "Let's sit here for a minute, Vicki. We've had no chance for a good talk since you've come."

She sat down willingly and waited with a sense of being happily at ease with him.

"I must admit," he went on quietly, "that I was disappointed to hear about your school marks. I can't understand how a girl with a mind as bright as yours could let herself fail."

The sense of happiness evaporated as swiftly as though it had never been. Vicki could feel herself stiffening to her very finger tips—the stiffening of resistance. So this was why he had lulled her with pretended friendliness. He was leading up to the moment when he could criticize and scold. He was as bad as Aunt Laura, who kept asking *why, why, why,* she had failed. It was such a silly question. How did she know why? Of course, in a way, she knew perfectly well. She had failed because she didn't study. Because she was thinking of other things, worrying about other things. And because once she had started being what people called a "problem," it was hard to stop. In fact, she wasn't sure she knew how to stop. But she couldn't explain any of this. She wouldn't even try. Instead of an explanation, the thing she had been so angry about yesterday rushed back to her mind, and she faced her father with the indignant words of a counter-attack.

"You needn't have told everybody! Why couldn't you let what happened stay back in America? Why did you have to tell Mrs. Byrne and Adria and Ken and everyone? They're all sneering at me and poking fun and laughing behind my back. Ken said he heard all about what a problem I was at home, and he said his mother was plenty worried about having me here."

She might have gone on if the sound of her own words and the look on her father's face had not frightened her into a silence that seemed to ring between them in the quiet garden. He was the stranger with a beard again—cold and stern. Remote, and most dreadfully polite.

He stood up and turned toward the house. "I have some work to do," he said. "Shall we go in now?"

It was all the worse to have him angry with her after the warm closeness she had felt toward him only a little while before. But it was her own fault for foolishly trusting that warmth and believing it to be real. She had always known that he wasn't like the fathers of other girls. He was so often shut away in his world of books and research, his writing and teaching. She should never have let herself be trapped into believing he cared about her problems.

They went indoors together and climbed the wide stairs in silence. When her father turned toward his room without a further word, Vicki stalked off to hers.

There were no lights on as yet in the big upstairs salon, and she almost stumbled over the figure that sat cross-legged in the recess of her door.

"I was waiting for you," Adria said. "I want to show you something."

Vicki was in no mood to be sympathetic toward Adria. "And I want to talk to you," she announced, pushing open the door of her room.

"You sound like Cousin Janet," said Adria, but she followed her into the room.

When Vicki had turned on the bed table lamp and closed the door so no one could hear, she faced the other girl.

"Did you put the little pin back?" she asked.

"How worried you are!" Adria smiled as impishly as Cemile. "I'll put it back as soon as I have a good chance."

For once Vicki felt she could understand Mrs. Byrne's viewpoint when it came to Adria.

"I looked for it in the garden this afternoon," she said. "When I couldn't find it I went to the sitting room to check whether you had put it back. Mrs. Byrne came in and found me there."

Adria clapped a hand to her mouth. "Was she very mad?"

"Mad enough. Anyway, I wish you would put it back before she finds out that it's missing."

Adria shrugged off Vicki's concern and took a few whirling steps around the room. Her answer came airily. "It wouldn't matter if Cousin Janet did think it was missing. I'd slip it back in a different place and when she came across it she'd believe she'd missed it the first time."

Vicki listened in growing alarm. If this was what Adria meant to do, there might be all sorts of trouble ahead. Anyway, it was sneaky and dishonest—even deliberately mean. Which seemed rather strange because Adria, for all her unexpectedness, did not seem like a mean person. There was something here she did not understand.

With a last whirl, Adria came back to her like a ballet dancer about to take a bow. She was smiling again but in an almost coaxing way.

"Don't be angry with me, Vicki. You're my only friend. You don't know how much I've looked forward to your coming. I thought you'd like me—because you were another girl and perhaps in trouble too. I didn't expect you to be superior and disapproving."

There was something winning about Adria, something a little heart-catching too. When Vicki remembered the terrible thing that had happened to her, she could not blame her very long for anything. She smoothed the frown from her forehead.

"Dad said he would take us to Istanbul Saturday morning," she said, though she was no longer sure her father would keep that promise. Or if it would be a happy occasion if he did. "He said you could show me the bazaars while he was looking at tiles in a mosque."

Adria cheered up at once in her quicksilver way. "Will he really? That's wonderful! I know what we can do. This will make everything easy. I was wondering how to manage it."

Her words were far from reassuring. Goodness only knew what Adria had in mind now. But before Vicki could ask questions, she started toward the door, speaking over her shoulder.

"I want to show you something. Come along quickly—before it's too late," She opened the door and then turned back. "Do you have the *tespih* I gave you—that string of blue beads. Bring them along."

There seemed nothing to do but pick up the beads from a table and follow Adria into the hall. Vicki had no wish to ask why the beads were wanted, lest she be told again about the "evil eye."

"Come—come quickly!" Adria repeated and grasped her by the hand.

The long upper hallway stretched ahead dark and empty, but Adria seemed to know her way like a cat who can walk in the dark. She hurried the full length of the hall, and Vicki went along, her wrist caught firmly in Adria's surprisingly strong grip.

At the end huge double doors with carved panels reached nearly to the lofty ceiling, barring the entrance to the haremlik. Adria put a hand on the brass doorknob and opened the lower catch. The door squeaked and creaked, but no one came to see what they were about, and Adria pushed Vicki through and closed the door behind them.

Again they traversed an even darker hallway that opened at last into another wide salon, empty of furniture, the bare floor echoing to their steps. As everywhere else in the house, old floorboards creaked as they moved over them, until it seemed as though they could not possibly be walking the corridor alone. On each side of the hall were doors closed upon their own secrets and showing only blank faces as the two girls went by. Vicki had an uneasy urge to look back over her shoulder to see if any of the doors opened behind them.

In the salon, Adria moved from one French window to another, opening several of them toward the west, so that the pale pink light of sunset came through the balcony arcades, bathing the room in a gauzy veil of color. As if appearing from nowhere, the lithe body of a tiger cat slipped past them into the house and streaked down the hall.

Vicki found herself standing in the pink glow, the beads clutched tightly in her fingers, while prickles crept along her spine. It was strangely eerie here in these deserted rooms.

"Can't you feel them all about us?" Adria whispered. "Such lovely silks the women wore. Not Turkish trousers the way you see in old pictures. Not in this house. This pasha would have sent the beautiful silks to Paris to be made into gowns. If you listen, you can almost hear high heels clicking in and out of the rooms—though I expect they still wore slippers for everyday. But you won't see a single hat. Because when they went out of the house, out of their own garden, the ladies put on a çarşaf—a hideous long black garment that covered them from their heads to their toes. And they wore a silk peçe to hide their pretty faces, all but their eyes. Imagine living shut up in these rooms and never unveiling their faces before any man outside those of the family. The word 'harem' means privacy, you know."

Adria managed to make the former occupants of the house seem so near and real that Vicki would hardly have been surprised if a Turkish lady had reached out of the gloom to pluck her by the sleeve.

To free herself of this feeling, she stepped through one of the French doors onto the wide balcony that ran across the end of the house. She felt better out here looking through arches that framed the garden. In the west, a pink tinge blended into saffron and aquamarine, with the rounded hilltop above rising in black silhouette against it.

"How did the women of Turkey happen to stop wearing veils and hiding themselves in harems?" she asked.

"Mustafa Kemal did that," Adria said. "Ataturk was the name they gave him after the last sultan was deposed, and he became the first president of Turkey. Father of the Turks, it means. He made a law that the veil and the fez had to go. He brought Turkish women out of the haremlik and educated them because he wanted Turkey to develop and grow more like the Western world."

Vicki glanced over her shoulder toward the dark, whispery rooms from which the light was fading.

"It must have been very sudden. Did they like it when it happened?"

"My father said lots of people didn't. But it was right after the First World War, and Turkey had been badly beaten fighting on the side of the Germans. Kemal stepped in and saved the country. So what he said had to be done. He was a dictator but not like the wicked ones. He is dead now, but you'll see his picture everywhere, and monuments built to honor him. Turkey has been a part of the modern world for only forty years or so, and some of the old ways and old things are still about."

With Adria in this pleasant, informative mood, Vicki felt better able to talk to her. She held up the blue beads.

"What is a—a *tespih?*"

Adria took the beads and slipped them through her fingers one by one. "Cousin Janet calls them fidget strings. Mother nicknamed them nervous beads. The Moslems have prayer beads, much longer than this. But now you'll see these short strands everywhere, and they have nothing to do with religion. Men run the beads through their fingers, play with them to give their hands something to do. Watch them and you'll see."

"But the blue color?" Vicki persisted.

"I told you. Evil spirits are distracted by blue and don't see the wearer, so the evil eye is kept away. Didn't you see the bandeau of blue beads Cemile wore in her hair? These *tespihs* come in all colors though. Sometimes they're made of fine amber instead of glass."

The light was fading quickly now, and Adria began to close windows and shutters. Vicki did not want to return through those rooms in complete darkness, but first there was something she must say to Adria.

"Tell me," she began a little breathlessly, "was it you looking down at Ken and me through the harem shutters a while ago?"

Silvery laughter mocked her and for a moment she thought the other girl would not answer. Then Adria nodded.

"I didn't think you could see me."

"I wasn't sure. Unless there was a shadow. But I had a feeling of eyes watching me. I thought it was you."

The other girl regarded her with interest. "Maybe you've got second sight, like Leyla."

"Oh, for goodness' sake!" Vicki cried. Adria was off again. Vicki started back through the shadowy salon of the harem ladies, meaning to stride firmly through the room and the hallway, back to the lived-in part of the house. But facing the darkness, she found she did not want to traverse the long expanse alone.

Adria must have sensed her hesitation, for she took Vicki's hand and walked close to her as they felt their way through dark echoing rooms together.

"Can you hear them?" Adria's voice was low. "They whisper and rustle their silks whenever I go through, as if they didn't approve of my coming here. But I think they're curious too. They're talking about us now in Turkish."

The tiger cat slipped out to join them, and Vicki

reached the big double doors on a run. Adria came after her, laughing in amusement.

"You were frightened in there, weren't you? Really frightened!"

The selamlik part of the house had been lighted in their absence. At the sight of illumination, Vicki's courage returned and with it her indignation.

"Don't be so silly!" she told Adria. "And don't change the subject. Why were you spying on us through the shutters?"

Adria tossed her head, and once more soft fair hair drifted lightly about her shoulders. "I wanted to know something. That's all."

"You mean you wanted to know how Ken was taking the mean trick you played in his workshop—is that it?"

They had paused in the hallway before Adria's room, and she stopped laughing abruptly and gave Vicki a strange, long look. For an instant it seemed as though there were tears in her eyes, shining in the lamplight.

"Thanks for coming with me, Victoria," she said, and there was a certain dignity in the way she spoke. She went into her room and closed the door behind her, leaving Vicki staring blankly.

Adria had not admitted the trick in Ken's workshop, but she had almost cried when Vicki had asked her about it. What was wrong here? What was Adria up to?

# 8

# Captain of the "Pinafore"

The next few days passed quietly enough. Dad mentioned Istanbul again in Adria's presence, so the plans for Saturday held. He was still remote, however. It wasn't that he seemed angry or critical but more as if he had dismissed the role of being a father and was once more busy with his own absorbing work. Vicki found herself haunted by an unexpected regret. Unpleasant though it might have been, she almost wished she had faced up to a real talk about her failure in school. Yet whenever she considered doing this, she shrank from what it would mean. How could she talk to that stranger who was so terribly clever that he would never have failed at anything himself, and who would be anything but patient with a daughter who had behaved stupidly? If Mother had been well, Vicki could have talked to her. But there was no one else, and she continued to bottle everything up inside herself, where it sometimes broke out in bad temper, like a small volcano.

At least nothing at all happened about Mrs. Byrne's pin that resembled the Golden Horn. Whether Adria had put it back in its place or not, Vicki did not know and did not try to find out. She kept her distance from the Turkish sitting room, never so much as passing close to the door. Adria did not mention the pin, and Mrs. Byrne had not shown it to anyone lately, or, for all Vicki knew, looked at it herself. So no trouble had blown up in their midst.

Having finally caught up on her sleep, Vicki found herself wakening early to the sounds of a Turkish morning—the crowing of cocks and bleating of goats, the calls of street vendors who climbed the hill to sell their wares to suburban families. Among these were yogurt sellers, vendors of crusty bread rings sprinkled with sesame seed, fruit sellers, and many others. On every hand, little don·keys carried double baskets in which were packed various wares, with men or women riding sideways on their sturdy backs.

During Vicki's fourth morning, Mrs. Byrne made a suggestion. "I'm driving toward Arnavutkoy this morning, if you'd like to come with me. That's a little village where there are Albanian fishermen, below the school that Adria attends. I'll drive you into the grounds and leave you there. You can take a lunch and wander around. Perhaps meet some of the girls during the noon hour. Then if you want to, you can look for Adria and get permission to visit one of her classes."

The plan sounded interesting, and she thanked Mrs. Byrne for thinking of it.

The early-morning mists had cleared from the Bosporus, and the day had lost its early chill, so that by noontime Vicki was comfortable without a sweater. The Bosporus had turned bright blue under a blue sky. Across it the mosques and palaces shone in the sun, and the hills of Anatolia rolled gently away. Real mountains were far off in the interior and could not be seen from here.

A gatekeeper let them into the school grounds, and Mrs. Byrne drove up a long winding road through thick woodlands and grassy banks, where goats were to be seen cropping. High on the hillside above, several white build-ings gleamed against greenery, the largest one with marble pillars across its face and thick wisteria spilling over the front door.

"That's the American Girls' College, where your father teaches," Mrs. Byrne said, pulling up in a parking place. "It's a very old school, started originally by a New En-gland educator. Well-to-do Turkish families send their daughters here to learn English and receive a modern edu-cation."

"But if it's a college, how does Adria happen to—"

"She goes to the prep school for younger girls," Mrs. Byrne said. "You can take that walk uphill from here and if you bear to the right, you'll reach the school for younger girls. Everyone will be outdoors at noon on such a nice day, so don't hesitate to ask directions. I'm sure you'll find girls who will know Adria. There aren't many American girls in the school this term."

Vicki picked up the string bag in which she had packed her lunch, a thermos of milk, and a book, in case she wanted to sit under the trees and read. She planned to stay for the afternoon and drive home with her father.

When Mrs. Byrne had gone, Vicki chose a path that mounted to the upper roadway. It was already past noon, and girls who had finished their lunch were wandering about the many paths that wound through the woods. What a lovely, lovely place for a school! She could hear nightingales again as she walked along, and when she smiled at the girls she passed, they smiled back rather shyly. No one spoke to her, however, and she felt hesitant about addressing any of these strangers.

Not that they looked any different from the girls back home. Most of them had dark hair, though some were blondes. They wore their hair in pony tails, or short bobs, or any of the other styles she might see at home. All were dressed in the school uniform of blue jumper, white blouse, and maroon jacket. Short socks and black shoes seemed to be the rule. The one difference she noted was that many of the girls wore tiny earrings of plain gold or set with little stones of coral, in earlobes that had probably been pierced.

She was contented enough to wander by herself and not inquire at once for Adria. If she came upon her, all right. If not, this was a fascinating place in which to walk as she pleased.

Following one woodland road aimlessly, she found the path climbing until she came into the open on a wide, grassy field sprinkled with tiny daisies. This must be a place where games were played. The field formed the flat crown of a high hilltop and the view was wonderful. Vicki walked along a circling path that edged a rocky cliff plunging downward to the road below. Beneath the road were the roofs of houses and at last the blue path of the Bosporus at the lowest level. From here the strait looked like a river, winding past small inlets and bays.

A low stone wall rimmed the cliff, and near it was a bench beneath a twisted tree. A perfect place to have her lunch, Vicki decided. She sat on the bench and took out her sandwiches, eating contentedly and watching the constant boat traffic along the waterway far below. From a nearby hill, a high sweep of power lines ran from the top of a great steel tower across to the other side.

She had just finished eating when four girls in school uniforms approached the rock wall not far from Vicki. They did not notice her under the tree. The three younger girls sat on the wall, and the older one began to stride up and down before them in a strange, swaggering manner. Vicki forgot the view and watched in astonishment.

The performer was a rather plump Turkish girl with short, curly black hair and big dark eyes that flashed with seeming indignation as she stamped back and forth on the grass. Once she twirled an imaginary mustache and addressed an imaginary companion as "Josefin'."

The younger girls giggled and rocked back and forth on the wall, dissolving in mirth. At once the older girl stepped toward them, her brows drawn fiercely down, her arms folded sternly across her body. The giggles quieted and when the girls were still enough to suit her, the performer began to sing. Her voice was clear and true, and low enough on the scale so that it was evident that she was cast in the role of a man. She sang out boldly, and Vicki caught the words.

> "I am the Monarch of the Sea,
> The Ruler of the Queen's Navee—"

Vicki realized she was rehearsing a part for the performance of *H.M.S. Pinafore* that Adria had mentioned. She listened until the song was finished and then left her place and started toward them. "That was wonderful," she said. There was sudden silence. All four girls turned and stared at her. The one who had been singing the part of the captain seemed taken aback for a moment. Then she recovered herself and smiled at Vicki.

"Thank you very much," she said.

The rehearsal was apparently over, and Vicki walked toward the older girl with interest. This was the first Turkish girl she had met, and she seemed ready to be friendly.

"My name is Vicki Stewart," she said. "My father teaches at the Girls' College. You speak English, don't you?"

"But of course," the girl said readily. "At school we are permitted to speak only English. I am Meral Kirdar." She pronounced her first name Mey-rahl, with the accent on the second syllable. "You must be the friend of Adria March, who is in my class at school. She is my friend."

Meral glanced at a gold watch on her wrist and gestured to the younger girls.

"It is late. You must go back now. I will escort the visitor."

"Thank you," Vicki said. "Do you think I could visit Adria's class this afternoon?"

"But of course," Meral repeated what seemed to be a favorite phrase. "Come, I will show you the way."

As they walked along, the Turkish girl gave her a quick, bright glance from time to time, as though she noted her dress, her hair, everything about her.

"What a good voice you have," Vicki said. "You should be fine as the captain of the *Pinafore*."

Meral seemed pleased. She was very pretty when she smiled and not a bit like the stern British officer she had been portraying.

"You have seen this play in America?" she asked. "You think I will not disgrace in the part?"

"Of course you won't," Vicki assured her. "You'll be very good."

"This I hope," said Meral soberly. "It is great responsibility, I think. My mother and my aunt will come to see, and I must not fail."

"I know how you feel," Vicki said. "I remember one time when I was acting in a school play, and I had my mother and four aunts all coming to see me. I was scared to death."

"I too will be—as you say. But it is my teacher I must not fail. She chooses for me this part. She says: 'Meral, you will make the wonderful, dramatic captain. And the voice is fine for this part.' So—I *must* be success. That is why I come to the Plateau everyday to practice my part."

"The Plateau?" Vicki asked.

"Is name for that place. It is like big stage, I think. So I shall not be—scared to death—on smaller stage in our school. Perhaps you will come to see *Pinafore*? We give only some songs, of course. We have not time for all."

"I'd love to come," Vicki said promptly.

They had left the field well behind and were following a path through the woods toward the school buildings. Vicki tried to think of more things to ask Meral before they reached the school and she would have to be silent.

"Do you know Adria well?" she inquired.

The Turkish girl nodded, serious now, even a little sad. "But of course," she said again. "She is my friend. My parents and her parents also are—were friends. When I think of Adria, sometimes I cry."

To Vicki's surprise the tenderhearted Meral thereupon cried, tears of sorrow running down her cheeks. She dabbed them away with her handkerchief.

"But now I must go back to class. You would like to see our library?" Meral asked.

Thus it was that Vicki, a little confused, found herself escorted into the small white school building and led upstairs to the library. Here Meral presented her to the American librarian.

"My class is now English," Meral said to Vicki. "After comes art. You will visit us then. Is more interesting."

And away she went, hurrying a little lest she be late.

The librarian smiled at Vicki. "I know your father," she said. "I'm happy to meet his daughter. It's fine that you've made the acquaintance of Meral Kirdar. She is one of our best students—and a good friend to have. Turkish girls are wonderfully loyal when they like you. Suppose you sit at the table here, and I'll get you a book about Turkey."

The library was a pleasant room, with windows opening on green treetops and a blue sky. In a moment the librarian had returned from the book stacks and set a small volume before her. Vicki turned to the beginning and read.

She had to skip a little in order to finish before the period was up. The sounds of voices and of girls moving about the halls told her that classes were changing. It sounded very much like school at home. Vicki returned the book to the librarian and was shown the way to the art room, upstairs in the very eaves of the building.

Girls trooped into this room eagerly and went at once to get their materials and find their places. Adria noted Vicki as she came in and gave her a rather strange look, almost as if she had never seen her before. Without speaking, she went to her place at a table where she was working on a small model room made of cardboard.

Meral smiled and nodded at Vicki as she came in, more friendly than Adria.

The art teacher said Vicki might move around the room if she liked and look at the work the girls were doing. The present assignment was to make a model of some room they had seen and admired.

The art room was big, with light pouring in from dormer windows set in deep recesses. As Vicki went quietly from table to table, the girls glanced at her with interest and some of them smiled as they showed her what they were doing. But though she looked at their artistic creations with admiration, she kept thinking about Adria and wondering, too, why Adria seemed deep in gloom this afternoon and hardly friendly toward her. Now and then she glanced across the bent, absorbed heads of the art class to the table where Adria sat working, looking at no one, a downcast expression on her face.

For school, Adria tied her hair high at the top of her head and let it fall away in a long pony tail as light and silky as the gold of a corn tassel. But Vicki remembered the way she looked at home with it floating about her shoulders, dancing as she moved, lifting lightly.

Edging her way around the tables to the place where Adria sat, Vicki slipped onto a stool next to her. As she sat down, a nightingale sang its lovely, whistling song in the woods outside, but none of the Turkish girls looked up. Undoubtedly they were all quite used to nightingales. Only Adria raised her head and listened with her heart in her eyes, as though the bird song was for her alone, as if she alone understood what the bird was singing. For a moment something of the gloom lifted from her face.

Vicki leaned forward on her stool to examine the room Adria was making. It seemed to be the interior of a palace. There was a low, thronelike divan against one wall, and she had painted rich hangings and even made a little Oriental rug for the floor.

A girl across the table from Adria noted Vicki's interest and bent toward her.

"She makes room of the seraglio," she whispered. "Very beautiful room in palace where sultan keeps many ladies."

Adria sat back from her work with an impatient gesture. She stared at the cardboard model for a moment as if it displeased her thoroughly. Then, before Vicki suspected what she intended, she raised one hand and smashed the whole thing flat with a blow, which could be heard throughout the classroom, and burst into tears.

At once the class fell into a shocked silence. The teacher turned in surprise, not knowing what was wrong. "What has happened?" she asked.

The girl across from Adria stood up. "She breaks the seraglio. She is very sad. She is crying."

"Thank you, Selma," the teacher said and came quickly to Adria. She took her gently by the arm, and Adria did not resist but allowed herself to be led away from the other girls and into the hall.

# 9

# Discovery

At once a buzz of whispering stirred through the room. The girls were all talking excitedly, some of them in Turkish, forgetting that they were to speak only English at school. But they were not laughing or making fun of Adria's outburst. They seemed sorry and sympathetic. Indeed, one or two were weeping softly because their tender hearts bled for Adria in her painful loss of both parents.

Meral, who moved with more assurance than some of the girls, hurried to Vicki.

"Perhaps you will go with her," she said. "You are her friend."

"I don't know if she wants me," Vicki said doubtfully. "She didn't seem at all glad to see me when I came in."

"With Adria one does not know," Meral said. "It is better if you go with her now."

Thus bidden, Vicki walked through the whispering, lamenting girls and stepped doubtfully into the hall. The teacher was talking to Adria, who seemed to have stopped crying, and she looked at Vicki in relief.

"I'm afraid Adria isn't feeling well. Since you live in the same house, do you think you could take her home? Or if you wait till school is out, perhaps Mr. Stewart will drive you both home."

It was decided, without much help from Adria, that it might be best to wait for Vicki's father to drive them home. Adria said she was all right, and she was sorry about breaking her model. But she didn't want to go back to the art room.

There were only a few girls in the library, and they went there to wait until school was out. Adria brought her schoolbooks and pretended to study, though Vicki suspected that she merely wanted to escape all questions and sympathy. Vicki chose a book to read and tried to follow the adventures of some English boys and girls on holiday in Scotland.

At the moment, however, her own Turkish adventure seemed far more interesting, and she found herself remembering with a sense of unbelief, that only last week she had been at home in America hating with all her might the prospect of being shipped off to Istanbul. True, she wasn't any happier here than she had expected to be, and all sorts of things were wrong. But she was interested in what she had seen—the gypsies, these Turkish girls, the queer old house in which she lived. Even in Adria, aggravating though she might be at times. Vicki wished she might find some way to help Adria get her feet firmly upon the ground so that she would stop being pulled in different directions.

Her sympathy for Adria, however, was put to a severe strain before the afternoon was over. Dad drove them home. Usually he brought Adria to school in the morning, but if they left at different times, she walked the short distance home. Sometimes there were clubs that met after school, or Dad had to stay for a meeting. But that afternoon they all went together, picking Ken up on the way, since Ken's boys' school was nearer home.

Ken was not speaking to Adria very often these days. He had not accused her of the trick in his workshop—he simply ignored her. Which was all right at the moment, because it enabled them to drive home without any teasing remarks. Adria sat in silence beside Dad in the front seat, and Vicki was glad to be with Ken instead of with her father.

As they all walked into the stone-floored room of the pasha's house, they found Mrs. Byrne sitting on the rim of the fountain waiting for them. Her eyes were bright, and there was a patch of high color on either cheek.

"May I speak to you a moment, Vicki?" she said and walked toward the Turkish sitting room.

With a sinking feeling that seemed to drop her heart into her very toes, Vicki followed Mrs. Byrne. She knew perfectly well what was coming, and she paused in the doorway and looked back to see whether she could hope for help from any direction.

Her father looked puzzled, but he had started up the stairs. Ken stayed where he was, staring in open curiosity. Adria, who was the only one who could be of help, cast not even a backward glance but fled up the stairs as if she could not wait to get away.

What a traitor she was! Vicki thought. What a disgusting coward! She braced herself for whatever was to come and went into the sitting room to face Mrs. Byrne. After all, innocence was on her side. She had done nothing wrong, and she was not going to take the blame for Adria.

Clearly Mrs. Byrne was angry, but she was trying to control her temper.

"Do sit down, Vicki" she said. "My friends have always told me that girls are much better behaved than boys on the score of mischief-making. But I'm not finding that true. Ken can behave badly at times, I'm sure. But I know where I stand with him. I must confess that you and Adria leave me completely bewildered."

Vicki sat stiffly upon the very edge of a soft Turkish divan, wishing for a good hard chair beneath her. It was hard to brace yourself for trouble while being smothered in soft cushions.

Mrs. Byrne seemed to seek for the right words. "I would much prefer to keep this between you and me, my dear. There is no reason why your father has to be brought into the matter."

She waited, but there was nothing to say, and Vicki clenched her teeth and doubled her fists in her lap.

"This is very difficult," Mrs. Byrne sighed. "Vicki, has anyone ever told you that you would be quite an attractive girl if you wouldn't scowl and purse up your mouth in that sullen expression? If you go about looking like that, I'm sure no one will like you or care very much to know you."

Vicki deepened her scowl and increased the sullen droop of her mouth. In the face of such injustice, she didn't want to smile sweetly at her tormentor. She didn't care whether Mrs. Byrne found her attractive or not.

"Very well, then," Mrs. Byrne said. "We'd better get to the point of this interview at once. I will make no fuss about what has happened, and I won't tell your father about it if you will simply return the little gold pin you took from my collection the other day."

Vicki found her mouth so dry that no words would come. She moistened her lips with her tongue and swallowed hard.

Mrs. Byrne went to the corner cabinet and indicated an empty space Vicki had noted before. "This was where the pin was put before I found you in the room the other day. I want to replace it as soon as you can bring it to me."

Inside, Vicki found herself practically shouting. *I didn't take your pin! I didn't, I didn't! Ask Adria what happened to it! Don't ask me!* But not a word came out aloud. She stared at Mrs. Byrne in stony silence.

"I can understand how something like that might tempt you into taking it," Mrs. Byrne went on, keeping her temper by a mighty effort. "I expect all children take things that aren't theirs at one time or another. The fact that you've done this doesn't make you a thief, Vicki. Not if it never happens again. I'm sure you've been properly brought up and that you have a conscience. I'm sure you know right from wrong."

Vicki wanted to say, *I do, even if Adria doesn't,* but the silence between them deepened until Mrs. Byrne lost her last shred of patience.

"Very well—since this is your attitude, I'll give you one more chance. If the pin is not back in its place by tomorrow evening, I shall go to your father. That's all I have to say, Vicki."

She went to the door and held it open. Wondering what was the matter with her own tongue, Vicki strode angrily past her and ran upstairs. Why hadn't she told on Adria?

Why hadn't she at least announced the fact of her own innocence? Yet somehow she had not been able to bring
herself to speak.

Upstairs she stood before Adria's door and listened.
There was a breathless quiet within the room. No whim-
pering, no crying. Only a waiting silence. Vicki startled
herself by the loudness of her banging upon the door.

There was a scurrying sound as Adria ran to pull it
open in her face.

"All right, all right," she said. "You don't need to
break the door down."

Vicki stalked into the room, and Adria regarded her
warily, as though she had let in some sort of wild animal
and didn't know whether or not to run for cover.

"What a thundercloud face!" she said.

"If one more person makes a remark about my face,"
Vicki said, "I'm going to—to—"

Adria dashed across the room and flung herself upon
the big bed with a flying leap. "Whatever it is, you
won't!" she cried. "I can move faster than you can, and
I'd never be there to catch."

Vicki found herself shaking in a perfectly disgusting
way. She went to a chair and sat down so that Adria
wouldn't guess.

"Are you going to give the pin back?" she demanded.

"So it *was* about the pin," said Adria. "I thought it
would be."

"Then why did you let her accuse me of taking it? Why
didn't you come down to her right away and give it to
her, so I wouldn't be in trouble?"

To Vicki's surprise, Adria's lower lip quivered, but she
blinked hard and did not let herself break down again.

"I'm sorry," she said. "Truly I didn't mean to get you
into such trouble, Victoria." She slid off the bed and
stood up. "I wanted a little more time to think. But I'll go
down now and tell her that I was the one who took the
pin."

In an unexpected flash, Vicki knew why she had kept
silent. Without thinking consciously at the time, she knew
deep inside her that it would be far worse for Adria to be

in this trouble than for Vicki Stewart. After all, her own
innocence could be explained to those who mattered most.
Whereas Adria was going to live with Mrs. Byrne for the
rest of her growing-up years and would now have an even
blacker shadow over her than any she had moved under
before.

"You needn't do that," Vicki said, her indignation fading. "Mrs. Byrne said I could put the pin back quietly and
nothing more would be said. If it's in its place by tomorrow night, she won't tell Dad, or say anything more about
it. So why don't you give it to me and let me put it back?
Your Cousin Janet doesn't need to know it was you who
took it."

The color drained from Adria's face. With no sunlight
to brighten them, her eyes were a dark, stormy gray.

"I can't give it to you!" she said tragically. "I can't return it because I haven't got it. I've looked and looked in
the garden, and I can't find it at all. That's why I smashed
my model in art class today and behaved in such a ridiculous way. I kept thinking about the awful thing I'd done,
and I couldn't find any way out."

This was worse than Vicki had expected. "You can't
have lost the pin, Adria. You had it right there in the garden. Do you suppose those gypsies—?"

Adria shook her head in a firm negative. "I know what
you're thinking—that gypsies steal. And I suppose they
do, some of them. They were outcasts in the old days, and
that was the only way they could live. But when a gypsy
is your friend, he doesn't steal from you. And these gypsies are my friends. They were my father's friends and my
mother's. Nothing would make them hurt me like that."

"Then the pin is down there in the garden still, and
we'd better look for it. Between the two of us, surely we
can find it."

Adria shrugged. "I don't think so. I'll go and tell Mrs.
Byrne what has happened."

She was halfway to the door when Vicki jumped up
and caught her by the arm. "No—wait! Let it go for now.
We've got until tomorrow night to find the pin. I don't
mind if she thinks for a little while that I'm to blame."

"Tomorrow is Saturday," Adria said. "We're going to Istanbul with your father tomorrow. We won't be home."

"That's right. So let's have a pleasant trip without any scolding and accusations. All we need to do is wait until tomorrow evening and then tell Mrs. Byrne before she goes to Dad. That is, if we haven't found it in the meantime. But right now we'll go down to the garden and comb every inch of grass around the place where you thought you put it. Perhaps you picked it up without remembering and then dropped it somewhere else."

"In that case, there's the whole garden to look through. That's impossible."

"We won't give up," Vicki said stubbornly. "We'll go down now and search as hard as we can."

That was what they did, crawling on their hands and knees in the grass, searching in a wider circumference than before, but finding nothing in spite of their efforts.

Adria was willing to talk about her feelings at last. "I never meant anything like this to happen. I'm not a thief, and I wouldn't play a trick that would hurt Mrs. Byrne like this. I know she prizes that pin. I only meant to borrow it to show Leyla, because of the Golden Horn shape. But if I can't return it, she really will think it has been stolen. Better me than you, since I'm the one who's to blame."

Vicki no longer considered her a coward, but she did wish Adria hadn't done such a foolish thing to start with. Even the borrowing of the pin would be hard to explain to Mrs. Byrne and losing it was inexcusable.

They were now exploring the edges of the weed-grown path by which they had made their way through the old part of the garden, searching the very earth to see if the pin could have been dropped and stepped on so that it was pressed into the dirt. They were concentrating so thoroughly that Ken's voice startled them. Adria looked up from a clump of weeds she was examining, and Vicki sat on her heels to stare at him.

"What are you two after? Buried treasure?" he asked. His red hair was tousled as usual, and his blue eyes were teasing.

"None of your business," Adria said.

"O.K., if that's the way you feel," said Ken. "But there's something else that is my business. And I mean the mess you made of my workshop the other day."

Adria rose from her knees and regarded him defiantly. "I didn't hurt anything," she said.

So it had been Adria, Vicki thought. What a shame!

"You made a lot of extra work," Ken told her. He wasn't teasing now. "If Vicki hadn't helped me, it would have taken a lot longer to straighten things up. If you do anything like that again, I'm going to turn you over to Mom."

"Why don't you tell her about me now?" Adria demanded. "Go ahead and see if I care!"

"Oh, no!" Vicki put in unhappily. Adria had very little sense. She was in enough trouble without adding to her difficulties.

Ken's grin was only for Vicki. "If *you* don't want me to, I won't," he said, and walked away through the garden.

Vicki stared after him in surprise, but Adria seemed plainly annoyed. "Now what did you do that for?" she snapped at Vicki.

"Because you're in all the trouble there is already," Vicki said impatiently. "This pin business is awful enough without Ken telling about the trick you played in his workshop."

"But don't you see that the two things are different?" Adria asked, and there was a pleading note in her voice. "One I meant to do—but it didn't actually hurt anything. I didn't mean to lose the pin, and that is hurting someone badly."

For the second time that day Vicki found herself completely confused. "Why would you want to mix things up in Ken's workshop? What harm has he ever done you?"

There was mockery in Adria's laugh, and she did not answer the question.

Instead she went whirling off through the garden toward the house. The flutelike notes drifting back to

Vicki had no appeal for her at the moment. The only bright thing in this entire picture was the fact that Ken seemed to have accepted her as a friend. Because she had asked him not to, he would not tell his mother about Adria.

# 10

# In the Covered Bazaar

Soon after breakfast the next morning, they started to Istanbul in Dad's Volkswagen. To Adria's annoyance, and Vicki's secret pleasure, it was decided at the last moment that Ken was to go along. Ken, Vicki felt, might serve as a balance for Adria and hold her down to solid earth at least part of the time.

Surprisingly, Adria was in good spirits this morning, and if a reckoning lay ahead of her by nightfall, she did not seem to be worrying about it. After making a face of distaste at Vicki behind Ken's back, she accepted his presence with a good enough grace. That very fact left Vicki worried. She began to suspect that Adria had something up her sleeve.

Ken had brought his camera, and Dad stopped the car near an old Moslem cemetery so that he could get a few pictures. The morning was gray and cool, with a promise of rain, but Ken had fast film in his camera and was undeterred from his picture-taking.

The cemetery, rimmed by dark cypress trees, was a quiet, deserted place up a hillside from the Bosporus. While Ken took pictures and talked to Dad about his camera, the two girls walked through weeds and tall grass, examining curious headstones. Most of them were tall thin sticks of marble, topped by large, pumpkin-like marble knobs sculptured into scalloped designs. The stones tilted crazily from age, leaning in every direction, though originally all the headstones had faced toward Mecca.

"Why do they have those knobs on top?" Vicki asked.

Adria paused before one of the stones and made it a respectful bow. "Those are turbans. You can tell by the shape how important a man was. This stone is a big fancy, distinguished turban, so it probably marks the grave of a very important pasha. The sort of pineapple effect is for a woman."

Knowing these things made the neglected old cemetery all the more fascinating, and Vicki studied the marble turbans with new interest. But Adria's mind was on other matters. She came close to Vicki and spoke softly so the others would not hear.

"I know how to get rid of Ken. I have a plan."

Adria's plans were exactly what Vicki wanted to avoid.

"Don't do anything foolish," she pleaded. "Not today. I don't see why we have to be rid of him anyway."

"We have to because he might keep me from what I want to do. I've got to find a way—it's the only chance I have."

All this was disquieting and seemed to promise more trouble, but Ken and Dad were returning to the car, and as Adria followed them, Vicki could ask no questions.

The car turned away from the Bosporus on a short cut to the city and followed the crest of a hill. The gently rolling countryside was visible for miles around, its pattern almost always the same. Sometimes there were bare stretches of reddish earth, sometimes areas wooded with pines or stands of tall cypress trees.

Modern apartment buildings marked the outskirts of the city and before long they were driving through the European section in the direction of Galata Bridge, with old Istanbul rising ahead. Motor traffic was heavy as they moved toward the historic bridge across the Golden Horn. On the far side, the ancient city of Istanbul—Constantinople of old—climbed its hills in solid tiers of buildings. The Turks, Dad said, had dropped the old name because this was no longer the city of Constantine, the conquering emperor.

It was a gray city, surprisingly lacking in color, yet fascinating and beautiful because of its mounded silhouette broken by great mosque domes and the needles of minarets. Every mosque must have a minaret, and the more important ones had several. Dad pointed out the famous St. Sophia, which had been a church, then a mosque, and was now a museum. The beautiful Blue Mosque and the Mosque of Suleiman the Magnificent rose majestically above surrounding buildings in pyramids of domes.

On the peak of the nearest hill, a tall fire tower reminded one that Istanbul had once been a city of wooden houses, with fire always a frightening threat. Now no one was allowed to build in wood, and the old-fashioned houses were gradually disappearing.

They'd reached Galata Bridge, where camel caravans and men in all the splendid costumes of the East had once gone back and forth daily. The bridge rested on pontoons and was swung open only at dawn to allow boat traffic through. Its lower level was a street in itself, and Vicki looked down at men selling fish directly from boats that had just brought in their fresh catch.

Once they were across the bridge, the streets grew narrow and twisting. Dad found a place to leave the car, and they walked through an arched stone gate into the wide cobblestone courtyard of a mosque. Here there was no motor traffic, and those on foot walked back and forth freely. Vicki remembered her mistaken notions about Turkey before she had come here. These people were dressed like those at home, and most of the passers-by gave the Americans no second glance. This was a cosmopolitan city accustomed to foreigners from other lands.

Above the courtyard, rose the great dome of a mosque—its minaret startlingly thin and tall, when seen close at hand. A wide flight of shallow stone steps rose to a stone platform before the doors of the mosque, and Dad led them over to these steps.

"I'm going to be working in here for a while," he said, gesturing toward the mosque. "Adria, since you and Ken both know your way through the bazaars, suppose you take Vicki around. We can meet at these steps an hour and a quarter from now. Is that agreeable?"

The three young people nodded, and Vicki thanked her father when he gave her some lire to spend. This trip into

Istanbul had not been the companionable visit she had
imagined when he first suggested it. The matter of her
failure in school still stood between them, though Dad had
not referred to it again. Now he was clearly eager to get to
his investigation of tiles.

A paved walk beneath plane trees crossed the courtyard
to a second arched gate. The flags of the old Ottoman Em-
pire were set into the stone above, and Ken stopped to
take a picture of this gate. At once, several Turkish boys,
who were selling ball-point pens to passers-by, came over
to watch him and ask questions in Turkish. Adria explained that one of them had never held a camera in his
hands and wanted Ken to let him look through the viewer.

While Ken showed him how to hold the camera and
where to look, Adria pulled Vicki through a second arch
and on toward the entrance to the bazaar.

"Here's our chance! Do come along, and we'll leave
him behind."

Vicki held back unwillingly. "I don't want to do that,"
she said. "There's no reason to be mean."

Adria made a face but gave up her tugging, and in a
few moments Ken joined them, and they left gray daylight
behind and stepped into the electric lighting of a strange
world.

The long corridor in which Vicki found herself was
arched over with ancient stone, its surface scabrous and
peeling. The floor beneath their feet was of cement, and
on either hand were rows of tiny shops, each consisting of
a brilliantly lighted display window, a narrow door, and a
matchbox interior where the dealer waited for customers
and haggled furiously over his prices. Other stone cor-
ridors opened off the first one, with still others opening off
them and connecting with one another, until Vicki felt
that she had walked into a labyrinth from which they
would never find their way back to the mosque where
they were to meet her father.

Moving through this great covered bazaar that was like
a town in itself, they stopped before windows that interested them and wandered as they pleased. Vicki's eye was

caught by a window in which nothing but gold bracelets were heaped in gleaming pyramids.

"When a girl marries in the old Turkish way," Adria explained, "the number of gold bracelets she owns is important. That reminds me, I want to get a present for someone."

She chose a shop that displayed silver objects and went in to look at arm bangles. The one she bought was simple and attractive and not at all expensive. But Vicki wondered what child Adria meant her gift for, since the bracelet was so small.

In the crowds following the stone walks she noticed several women wearing voluminous trousers, their hair covered by a scarf.

"From the villages," Adria said, "where they're still old-fashioned. It was the custom that a woman must never let a man see her hair, so the village girls still cover their heads, like our Fatma at Cousin Janet's."

Ken was interested in shops of copper and brass, where handsome trays and vases and braziers were shown. But now Adria seemed in a hurry, and she urged Vicki along.

"Why don't you buy some Turkish slippers?" she suggested. "I know a shop where you can get nice ones, and the man won't charge you too much."

The idea of looking at slippers seemed to bore Ken, but he came along good-naturedly. On the way, however, the window of a small jewelry shop caught his eye. Vicki came over to look too. If she could find a duplicate of the horn pin, she would gladly buy it with the money Dad had given her. It might be a way to get Adria out of the trouble she would be in when Mrs. Byrne knew the truth.

Adria stood beside her, speaking in a low voice so Ken wouldn't hear. "I know what you're thinking. But even if we found a pin that was exactly like it—which isn't possible because all these things are made by hand—it would still be too expensive for us to buy. That was a very good piece. We'll have to try my way, Victoria. Do come along and see the slippers."

The slipper shop was around two more corners, and Adria pushed her way through several women who were making purchases and went to the back of the shop. She greeted the dealer in Turkish. He was friendly, making Vicki a very polite bow, and addressing Adria as *Kuçuk Hanim*, which was a form of respect for a young lady.

"Turkish people like Americans," Adria told her. "They know we're their friends. Pick out a pattern you like, and the dealer will give you the slippers in your size."

There were rows and rows of handmade Turkish slippers in all sorts of colors and weaves. Some were velvet, some bright multicolored cloth coarsely woven, some were embroidered, and some turned up at the toes with big pompons on the end. All had sturdy leather soles. It was difficult to choose, and Adria was no help because she was so critical. When Vicki decided on a pair she liked, Adria would at once find another pair more attractive or show her what was wrong with the ones she had selected.

Ken had come in with them, but after a few minutes of this, he began to fiddle with his camera. When Adria vetoed Vicki's sixth choice, he started for the door.

"No use waiting here," he said. "I'll go outside and try for a time shot of the bazaar street. You can look for me around the corner."

No one objected, but the moment he was gone, Adria's eyes began to dance with excitement.

"I knew we could wear him down," she said in triumph. "Why don't you take that red pair with the pompons?"

It was unreasonable to be hurried after all this delay, but since Vicki liked the red pair, she agreed. She tried on her size, paid the dealer the very reasonable amount he asked, and let Adria pull her to the door.

Outside, Ken was nowhere in sight. Adria slipped a hand through her arm and drew her toward an exit door at the far end of their corridor. When she saw what was intended, Vicki held back objecting, but Adria pleaded with her earnestly.

"Do come—please! You won't be sorry. We'll be back in plenty of time to meet your father, and Ken won't care.

He'll be glad to be rid of us so he can do whatever he wants. Besides, if you don't come with me, I'll go alone."

This, at least, Vicki could prevent. She did not mean to let Adria out of her sight.

The exit they stepped through was not the gate by which they had entered, but one of the numerous doors that opened from different sections of the covered labyrinth. In a moment they were out in gray daylight again, and Adria turned up a steep narrow street of cobblestones with an air of knowing exactly where she was going.

The tiny sidewalk, paved with uneven stones, was so rough that it was easier to walk in the street like everyone else. Following Adria uneasily, Vicki dodged around a water seller who was doling out cups of water poured from the spout of a copper jar. The rain still held off, and every gust of wind carried the dry smell of dust-laden air.

As Adria hurried her along, Vicki felt the strangeness of old Istanbul all around her. This was an old, old street, crumbling into shabby ruin. Yet, the people they passed were friendly and courteous, and Adria moved among them with the assurance of familiarity.

Not until they reached a stretch of aged wooden houses set back from the street no more than a foot or so by the narrow sidewalk, did Adria pause and look anxiously up at overhanging balconies. Some still boasted the perforated latticework of harem shutters. The houses were three stories high and very narrow, their wooden fronts unpainted and weathered to a darkening brown.

Suddenly Adria pointed. "There it is!" she said and darted across the street under the very nose of a donkey who wore a necklace of blue beads to keep him safe from the evil eye. Vicki caught her breath and flew after her, escaping a possible nip.

"Where are you going?" she cried. "What are we doing here? How will we ever find the way back?"

Adria paid no attention to her questions. She opened a door in one of the houses and stepped into a dark hallway. A cat sprang out of her way as Adria started up a narrow flight of wooden stairs. Unwilling to be left behind, Vicki followed. Into the darkness they climbed, up and up steeply without seeing anyone. By the time they reached a small vestibule at the top, Vicki's eyes were accustomed to the gloom, and she avoided running into a stove on her way to a closed door. In the room beyond she could hear women talking and a girl's voice laughed aloud. The sound struck a chord or remembrance.

Quite suddenly Vicki knew who it was they had come to see.

# 11

# Adria's Plan

At Adria's knock, the voices within quieted. The door was opened, and the two girls stood blinking in a sudden flood of daylight from windows beyond.

The elderly Turkish woman who had come to the door stared for a moment in surprise. When she recognized Adria, she smiled delightedly, holding out her hand. Adria knew how to make a respectful, old-fashioned greeting. She took the wrinkled hand, kissed it, and put it to her forehead. Then she thrust Vicki forward, saying her name and speaking words in Turkish. Evidently the woman did not expect the same greeting from Vicki, for she merely shook hands with her in warm welcome.

All this took no more than a moment, and beyond their hostess Vicki noted a tall girl standing before the windows. The girl turned and rushed across the room in a whirl of colored beads and gay flowered skirts. She caught Adria by the shoulders affectionately and kissed her on either cheek. It was the gypsy girl, Leyla. As Vicki had guessed, they had come to the home of Leyla's nongypsy grandparents.

As the two Americans were drawn into the room, Vicki saw that it was large and square, with two big windows opening above the street. Since the harem shutters had been removed up here, daylight flooded through these third-floor windows. A big double bed, with a neat hand-woven spread upon it, stood against one wall, for clearly this was both bedroom and living room. A big stove of shiny green porcelain stood opposite the bed, with its tin pipe running to an outlet near the ceiling.

Very high on the wall several framed photographs had been hung, and among them Vicki noted the face of a girl who looked no older than Leyla and very much like her. Probably this was Leyla's mother, who had run away with a gypsy. There was also a mounted sketch of Leyla's head done in pencil. On the opposite wall hung the picture of a stern-looking man in uniform, whom Vicki guessed must be Ataturk.

The two guests were made welcome and seated in the best cushioned chairs. The grandfather, who had fought in the First World War, was introduced. He was old and lame and did not rise from his place in the corner, though be bowed to them in courteous welcome. Vicki noted the string of brown beads in his hands. As he listened to the buzz of voices going on about him, with his wife and Leyla and Adria all talking at once, he slipped the beads quietly, absently through his fingers.

Vicki began to suspect the reason why they were here. Adria must have decided that the gypsies had picked up the pin from the garden after all, and she had come to see if they could get it back. Now she was glad she had not opposed Adria, for recovery of the pin would solve a good deal.

Leyla's grandmother brought a bottle of fragrant cologne for her guests' refreshment, and Vicki followed Adria in sprinkling some on her hands and rubbing it in.

"Where is Cemile?" Adria asked, glancing about the room. "Is she outside playing?"

A silence fell upon Leyla and her grandmother, and they looked at each other sadly.

"Cemile has sickness here," Leyla said, and held her stomach graphically.

She beckoned to Adria and Vicki and moved to a door curtained in brightly flowered material. When she parted the curtains, Vicki saw a second, very small room where Cemile had been put to bed on a low cot. The little girl looked thinner and more frail than ever, but her big dark eyes opened wide at sight of them, and she smiled a delighted greeting.

Adria went to her at once and knelt beside the cot. "I've brought you something, Cemile," she said and gave the child the silver bangle she had bought in the bazaar.

Cemile's cry was one of pleasure as she held out her arm so that Adria could clasp it about her wrist. Now Vicki knew why Adria had chosen a bracelet so very small.

Cemile's eyes rested adoringly on Adria and followed her when she stood up. So that the child need not be excluded from the visit when they returned to the bigger room, Leyla wrapped a blanket about her small sister and picked her up in strong arms. She sat with the others, holding Cemile in her lap, with the child's dark head resting against her shoulder.

Leyla's grandmother hurried to the vestibule where the cooking stove was kept and prepared tea. She brought in small glasses of the hot brew set in delicate china saucers and passed around a plate of *locum*—the deliciously sweet confection known as Turkish delight.

As they ate and sipped, Adria motioned to the framed pencil drawing of Leyla's head, calling it to Vicki's attention. "My father did that sketch of Leyla. It's good, don't you think?"

It was good, catching as it did something of a wild gypsy beauty that had never been tamed by brief spells of city living. Her hair in the sketch had the same untamed look Vicki had noted on their first encounter. Today it was more neatly brushed—a concession undoubtedly to her grandmother's ways.

Adria put herself out to entertain her friends, and especially Cemile. She told about the pasha's house, where she lived, and of the dark, empty rooms that had once been the haremlik. She did a little imitation of Mrs. Byrne's despairing manner when things were going wrong, and Vicki had to laugh, even though the mimicry reminded her of the trouble that lay ahead unless Adria recovered the pin. She wondered how Adria could make fun of Mrs.

Byrne so lightheartedly, when an evening of reckoning still lay ahead.

Nothing was said, however, about the reason for Adria's visit, and she went on as though this was no more than a social call. When she found her audience laughing, she went on in a mixture of Turkish and English to tell them about the trick she had played upon Ken in his workshop and of how annoyed he had been.

Leyla and Cemile laughed at everything she said, but the old man in the corner was quiet. So was the grandmother now, and Vicki guessed that she might be putting herself in Mrs. Byrne's place. Since Adria was sensitive enough to catch this undercurrent of disapproval, she soon dropped her mocking account and held out her hand to Leyla.

"I've come for your help," she said. "Please tell me about the sign you saw in my hand and in Victoria's. You said the sign would help me and when I found it good things would begin to happen. I need to have good things happen soon, Leyla."

Oh dear, Vicki thought. Here they were back to fortunetelling again! When was Adria going to ask Leyla about the pin?

The gypsy girl's laugh sounded faintly embarrassed, and Vicki suspected an uneasiness in the quick look she threw her grandmother. The old man fiddled with his string of beads and drew down his bushy white eyebrows in an expression of disapproval. The grandmother shook her head gently as if she did not approve of Adria's request, but she did not interfere.

Leyla's hesitation lasted only a moment and then she gave Cemile to her grandmother to hold and once more took Adria's hand in her own. She drew her down upon the faded, but still beautiful carpet and sat with her legs crossed beneath gay gypsy skirts. The long strands of beads about her neck swung and clashed gently as she bent forward over Adria's hand. Once more her forefinger traced the lines upon Adria's palm, and she caught her lower lip between strong white teeth as though she were thinking earnestly. After a few moments she began to sway back and forth with her eyes closed, murmuring in a soft, faraway voice.

"I see place in very old garden," she chanted. "Garden where much happens in ancient time. I see steep hill and many stone walls. Is very quiet in this place. Golden Horn is here. You will find."

The old man in the corner did not understand the words his granddaughter spoke in English, but he clearly did not like what she was doing. He spoke out in quiet reproof, so that Leyla dropped Adria's hand and sprang to her feet.

"My grandfather does not like gypsy ways," she said. "When I stay in Istanbul I must be like gorgio—who are not gypsies. But soon Cemile goes with me to the hills, and we are Romany people."

Cemile began to cry fretfully, and the grandmother sighed and gave the child to Leyla, who carried her to the double windows that opened upon a balcony.

"May it pass," Adria whispered to Cemile. "May you be well again soon." Then she turned to Vicki. "Come here and see the balcony."

She stepped over the window sill, and Vicki followed her to stand upon the narrow wooden balcony far above the street. They could see up and down the twisting cobblestones and over lower rooftops down the hill—a sea of rooftops, age-darkened and patched, interrupted as always by mosque and minaret. Some strange earthen humps with openings in them rose from the roof of a nearby building. They marked what had once been the roof of a Turkish bath, Adria said.

Sounds of teeming life came up to them from below. Workmen hammering on sheets of copper on the street of coppersmiths a block over. The calls of street vendors, the cries of children, the braying of a donkey, and the barking of dogs—all mingled together.

Through the bedlam cut a clear American voice: "Hey, come on down, you two. We'll be late to meet Vicki's father.

In astonishment, they looked down into the street below the balcony to see Ken's red hair. He waved an arm at them and then stepped out of sight beneath as a car honked at him. Adria turned reluctantly back to the room.

"I suppose we'd better go," she said. "How do you think he found us?"

Vicki had no idea, but she supposed that they were in for still more trouble. As they returned to the room, she whispered anxiously to Adria.

"Ask her! Ask Leyla about the pin."

"Hush!" said Adria so fervently that Vicki was silent.

They said their good-bys hurriedly, and Leyla came with them to the upper landing. Away from the living room, Adria pleaded with her.

"You haven't told me enough, Leyla. Where is this garden? Where do I look for the spell that will change everything?"

Leyla laughed softly and seemed for a moment to be thinking. Then she said: "Nine is the number. Nine stones from the wall—that is the number."

But she would explain no more, in spite of Adria's further urging. "Go with smiles. And a safe return," she said in the Turkish manner.

On the way downstairs, Vicki was in a state of thorough exasperation.

"How silly can you get?" she snapped, remembering Ken's first description of Adria and agreeing with it wholeheartedly. "Couldn't you see that Leyla was making all that up? I don't think she can tell fortunes any more than I can. Why didn't you ask her if she had the pin? That was the important thing to know—not all this silly stuff about nine stones and old gardens."

The stairway was so narrow that she was talking to Adria's back as the other girl marched down ahead of her. Adria did not turn, but when she answered, her words were spoken as heatedly as Vicki's.

"Do you think I would insult good friends by asking a question like that? You keep out of my business after this. I know what I'm doing, if you don't."

They were furious with each other by the time they stepped into the street where Ken waited impatiently. He took one look at their faces and whistled.

"Looks like a fight. Who's winning?"

Adria glared at him instead of at Vicki. "How did you know where we were?"

"Followed you, of course," Ken said cheerfully. "Don't you think I knew you were waiting to be rid of me? I hope you can find your way back from this place, because I sure can't. Who lives up there anyway?"

Neither girl answered him. Adria took the lead, and Vicki followed a step or two behind, with Ken treading on her heels. In single file they threaded their way past narrow houses, past shops where all sorts of strange items were sold, past open courtyards where men seemed to be working busily at various handcrafts or mending pieces of machinery. About the courtyards crowded more tumbledown buildings with human beings crowded solidly into them.

At a crossing a boy darted by, carrying a brass tray suspended by triple chains, on which were balanced several small cups of black Turkish coffee. More than once they passed one of the numerous street fountains, where everyone came to drink and wash and get water for cooking.

Fortunately, Adria knew her way, and it wasn't long before they reached the bazaar, threading their way through it to the courtyard outside the mosque.

Dad was on the steps, watching the pigeons, and he smiled when he saw them.

"Hi, kids. Have a good morning? I was beginning to wonder what had happened to you."

Without understanding exactly how she knew, Vicki sensed that she and Adria and Ken had closed ranks. Ken would not tell about their running away from him. Adria would put on a cheerful face before Dad, and she herself would be silent about the visit to Leyla's grandparents. They might be angry with each other, and jointly annoyed with Ken, but they did not want to discuss all this with grownups at the moment.

As she climbed the steps, Vicki saw that a row of taps and a gutter trough ran along one side of the mosque. Here men were washing in what Dad said was the prescribed way of their religion. The hour of prayer was approaching.

"Vicki has never been inside a mosque," Dad said. "Let's show her this one."

They took off their shoes, carrying them in their hands as they stepped into the vast dim interior, vaulted over by the ceiling of the great dome. The floor was covered by thick layers of rich Turkish and Persians carpets, and their feet made no sound. Beneath the dome, electric light bulbs strung on wires dimly lighted a portion of the mosque. Toward the front, rows of men knelt, bowing toward Mecca and murmuring their prayers. Women did not come to the mosques and were not expected to.

"Come," Dad whispered, "let's go outside in time to catch the muezzin."

They returned to the courtyard and stood craning their necks at the tall minaret. Near the top the bulge of a tiny stone balcony circled it, and it was here the muezzin would stand. Inside this stone needle, Dad said, were a hundred and fifty stone steps winding round and round all the way up.

As they watched, a man appeared on the balcony, and Vicki remembered pictures she had seen in books of this ancient Moslem custom. This man wore no turban, no flowing robes, as she recalled from pictures, but was dressed in an ordinary business suit. He cupped his hands about his mouth, and a long haunting cry went out over the city. She could hear it only faintly as the wind blew it away, and she was aware of the minaret needle piercing a stormy sky that looked as though it might let down torrents of rain at any moment. All the liquid Oriental sounds of the call to prayer, with Allah's name echoing through it, rang out again, closer now as he turned in their direction.

"He is calling people to prayer," Dad said. "His cry is called the *azan*, and you'll hear it echoed five times a day from every mosque."

"Some of them use loud-speakers now," Adria put in. "But I like the old-fashioned way better. I can tell you the words of the call."

She closed her eyes, the better to concentrate, and spoke the words softly.

"God is the most great.... Come to prayer, come to salvation. ... There is no god but God. ..."

The cry above them rang out for the prescribed number of times, and then it was over, and the man disappeared.

"It's good to see how others worship," Dad said. "At one time the Turks would have resented visitors in their mosques, but people are growing closer these days, and there's no more talk about infidels. They make us welcome. I wonder if you know that Christ is revered by Moslems as one of the greatest of prophets and that they consider the Old Testament a sacred book."

The threat of rain was being fulfilled by a gray drizzle, and they cut through the shelter of the bazaars once more. Dad had brought his big umbrella, and when they stepped outside again, the two girls huddled under it, one on each side of him as they hurried along. Ken had a slicker in his camera bag and got into it quickly.

Almost at once, the dust that enveloped Istanbul and lay thick between the cobblestones, was whipped into slippery mud. The four stepped carefully as they walked in the street past the Spice Bazaar, where spices and nuts and coffee beans were sold in the open-faced shops. The fruit-and-vegetable market had an awning over it, and as they went past, the dealer prodded it from underneath with a long pole so that a stream of water flooded into the street with little regard for passers-by. Beneath the dripping awning, vegetables made a bright spread of color. Vicki glimpsed red tomatoes, green peppers, and slim purple eggplants, smaller than those in America.

"Not much farther," Dad said. "I thought we might have lunch at a restaurant here in the Spice Bazaar."

They ducked through a doorway and shook off the rain. He led the way to stairs leading to the top of a very old building. Here in a small room with decorative tiles all around the walls and windows that looked out upon busy Galata Bridge, they sat down at a table. Luckily there was an English menu, but Vicki let Dad choose her meal because even in English she wasn't sure of what some of the dishes were. The waiter was friendly and helpful and seemed used to waiting on foreigners.

"This is a very old and famous place," Dad said, "and the food is especially good."

Vicki still felt worried about what lay ahead and annoyed with Adria, but a little of the tension went out of her when the food was served, and she began to eat. There were thick squares of the delicious white cheese, beans cooked in oil and vinegar, swordfish right from the sea and broiled in small pieces on a skewer, a mound of pilaf.

Dad ordered a dish of tiny black olives that had a pleasantly bitter taste, quite different from the bland ripe olives at home. As usual there were lemon slices on the table, since Turks squeezed lemon juice on almost everything, adding an interesting flavor.

When Dad asked about their morning, Ken told of his picture-taking and Vicki mentioned the purchase of her Turkish slippers.

"Is that all?" Dad asked. "I thought you'd come home loaded down like a donkey with things from the bazaar."

"Mostly I just looked," Vicki said lamely.

Dad seemed a little puzzled by the restraint that suddenly lay upon the three young people, and he tried to keep some sort of conversation going. He had been saving a surprise for them, he said.

"Since you and Adria and Meral Kirdar seem to like one another," he told Vicki, "I've invited her over tomorrow afternoon. I saw her at school, and she mentioned that her parents were driving to Bebek to see friends, and I suggested that they drop her off at Mrs. Byrne's for a visit. I telephoned her mother, and she was agreeable."

Even Adria seemed pleased by this plan. "I like Meral," she said with enthusiasm. "She's more serious than some of the girls, but she's good fun too. She'll make a wonderful captain in *Pinafore*. I'm glad she's coming."

This plan could not include Ken because Turkish girls of Meral's age were not permitted to associate with boys not of their own family, but Ken said he had other plans for the day and wouldn't be home, so that did not matter.

Vivki could only hope that she and Adria would be speaking to each other by tomorrow.

They drove home through a misty rain, and for Vicki the threat of what evening held loomed more alarmingly than ever. Even Adria seemed thoughtful and subdued, but she gave no sign of what she meant to do, and Vicki would not ask her. She had been rebuffed by Adria too many times today. Before dinnertime, the drizzle had turned into a downpour, and there could be no hope of searching further in the garden.

When the meal was served, Vicki felt too jittery to eat very much, even though the meat cooked in vine leaves was delicious. She was aware that Mrs. Byrne watched her now and then in a pained, inquiring way.

When the meal was over, Adria left the table at once and went upstairs to her room. Vicki waited only long enough to see that Mrs. Byrne was going into her sitting room—undoubtedly to check on whether the pin had been returned. Then Vicki too ran upstairs and reached the other girl as she opened her door.

Adria was rather small and slight and when Vicki caught her by the arm and whirled her about, she did not try to resist.

"I've had enough," Vicki said. "After the way you've acted today, I don't see why I should take the blame for you any longer. You said you'd tell Mrs. Byrne the truth, and I think you'd better go do it."

Adria tried to laugh, but the effort was not very successful. "I've changed my mind," she said. "I've decided not to tell her after all. You do whatever you like. The whole thing is up to you."

# 12

# Dread Wakening

Speechless with indignation, Vicki stared at Adria
March. She found it hard to believe that she would not
come to her help now that the moment of reckoning had
arrived. Her worry had been more for Adria's problem
than for herself.

"Do you really mean—" she began.

Adria drew her arm from Vicki's grasp. "I really
mean!" she echoed. "You can tell her anything you like. I
didn't mean to lose her pin, and I'm sorry about that. But
now that this has happened, I might as well use it."

"Use it?" It was Vicki's turn to repeat.

"Oh, never mind. If I go nobly down and take the
blame, I'll seem like a sort of heroine in spite of everything. And that's one thing I don't want to be. I'm sorry
you're mixed up in this, but that can't be helped. You
shouldn't have gone snooping in that room to check up on
the pin. Since you did, you'll have to get out of this in
your own way. Go ahead and tell her about me—I don't
care."

Adria stood with her fair head flung back, and her
hands on her hips. Vicki could hardly believe what she
had heard. In spite of Adria's defiant expression, she
looked strangely sad, as if she were breaking her heart
beneath this outward defiance. Suddenly Vicki's anger began to fade.

"What will you do," she asked curiously, "if I save you
again and take the blame?"

Adria made an impatient gesture. "Don't do that!

120

There's no point in your playing heroine either. Tell her the truth. I took the pin, and I lost it in the garden."

"Is that what you want me to tell her?"

"That's what I want you to tell her," said Adria. She gave Vicki a quick look of warning. "Sh—here comes Ken."

Vicki looked around to see him approaching from the head of the stairs. He moved slowly as though he did not want to get anywhere very fast. When he saw the two girls in Adria's doorway, he approached them almost reluctantly.

"Mom wants you," he said to Vicki.

Adria gave her a little push out of the doorway. A push that said, "Go ahead and tell her," and Vicki found herself looking at Adria's closed door.

A trembling started inside her as she started for the stairs, and she wished herself anywhere in the world but here.

"Don't be scared," Ken said kindly. "Mom told me about the pin. If you took it, why don't you give it back to her? Mom's an awfully good sort. She won't tell your dad if you give it back."

"I can't give it back," Vicki said. "I haven't got it."

Understanding dawned in Ken's eyes. "Say—I'm beginning to get it! Adria is in on this, isn't she? I'll bet you never took that pin at all. I couldn't believe you'd do a thing like that."

Vicki quirked her eyebrows in a frown. "Don't forget that I'm supposed to be a problem. It's the sort of thing everyone expects me to do."

"Not me," he said. "Let's get this straight before you go down. Let's go talk to Adria."

His unexpected belief in her was comforting, and it strengthened her courage. Without answering she started down the stairs. Quite suddenly she was sure of two things: She knew what she would say to Mrs. Byrne, and she was filled with a growing belief that Adria, while she might have a strangeness about her, was neither whacky nor anything else of the sort. She was working out some sort of strange plan of her own, and there was a purpose behind everything she did. What that purpose was, Vicki could not guess. She knew only that she did not want to play into Adria's hand and do what she now expected her to do.

"Am I right?" Ken asked as he walked down the stairs beside her. "Because if I am, then I'm going with you and tell Mom that you're covering up for Adria."

This was the last thing Vicki wanted, even though she liked him for suggesting it.

"Thanks, Ken," she said. "But I want to do this my way. Please don't say anything. Not now."

Doubtfully, he walked with her to the door of the Turkish sitting room and let her go in alone.

Mrs. Byrne sat upon a cushioned divan, one arm resting on the window sill beside her as she looked out at the streaming rain. Vicki's feet made no sound on the Turkish carpet, and she had advanced to the middle of the room before Ken's mother turned and saw her. Somehow Mrs. Byrne did not seem as much an enemy as she had before. Indeed, she was smiling hopefully, as though she wanted this unpleasantness ended and forgotten as quickly as possible.

"Have you brought me the little gold pin?" she asked gently.

Vicki took a deep breath and put her hands behind her back, bracing herself for whatever was to come.

"I can't bring it back," she said as she had to Ken. "I haven't got it. I think it was lost in the garden, but though I've looked and looked, and Adria has helped me, we can't find it."

Mrs. Byrne pushed the pillows aside and sat up straight. "Why was it taken into the garden?" she asked despairingly.

"I don't know," Vicki said. "I—I guess it seemed like a good idea at the time. I'm sorry. If you'll give us a little more time, we'll search again. It's such a big garden."

"So big that you'd be looking for a needle in a haystack," Mrs. Byrne said. She sighed and stood up, moving undecidedly about the room. "I don't know what to say. I realize that you are already in a good deal of trouble, Vicki, and I don't want to make things worse for you."

Trouble? Vicki thought. Oh, about school. How far away that had begun to seem. She had been in Turkey only a little while, but so much had happened that she felt as though she'd been away from home for months.

"Incidentally," Mrs. Byrne went on when Vicki was silent. "I owe you an apology for mentioning your school difficulties to Ken and Adria. Your father wanted me to know what the situation was, since you would be more or less in my charge when you came here. But I wasn't thinking of how you might feel when I let them know."

Vicki gave her a surprised, relieved smile. So it hadn't been Dad's doing, after all. She had blamed him unfairly this time.

Mr. Byrne seemed startled by her smile, but after a moment's hesitation she smiled back.

"Let's leave the matter for now," she said. "Look in the garden, or wherever you were when you had the pin. And we'll hope that it will come to light. Now that you're willing to talk about it, I feel much better, Vicki."

"Thank you," Vicki said politely.

As she went out of the room she no longer felt like smiling. She was still shaky, though at least she had accomplished what she intended. She had not taken the blame openly, she had admitted nothing, but neither had she shifted the guilt to Adria. And she had made a gain in time. Granted time, they might still be able to retrieve the pin.

She found Ken sitting on the edge of the fountain. The stone-flagged room seemed cold with the rain pouring down outside. When he saw her he jumped up and came toward her.

"How did you make out?" he asked.

"All right," Vicki told him. "Your mother was nice about it."

"I knew she would be," Ken said. "It's just that she's used to boy trouble more than girl trouble. And you'll have to admit that Adria is a handful. Mom is pretty worried about our taking her home to the States. Did you tell her that Adria—"

Vicki shook her head firmly. "I didn't tell her anything. And I'm not telling you either. I don't know exactly what Adria is up to. Don't ask me any questions now, Ken."

"O.K.," he said cheerfully. "You can yell if you need help. In the meantime. I'll let it alone. Though if you're smart, you won't trust Adria for long."

They went upstairs together to the big salon, where Ken stood looking around for a moment.

"Do you know how to play chess?" he asked.

Vickii shook her head.

"Then I'll teach you," he decided. "There's a table over there with a chessboard set right into it. And I've got an ivory and ebony chess set that Dad and Mom gave me last Christmas. Dad is keen when it comes to playing chess."

He drew two chairs over to the small square table, opened a drawer in it, and began to set out the chessmen, showing Vicki where each one went on the board. Vicki picked up an ebony knight in admiration. The carving of the horse's head and mane were beautifully detailed, the body polished to a sheen.

When the two armies were arrayed on each side of the board, waiting for the battle to begin, Ken had a wonderful idea. From a corner of the room, he drew out a big brass *mangal*—a brazier like the ones Vicki had seen in the bazaars. It was brightly polished and resembled a great open flower, with charcoal ready to be lighted in its heart. Ken found matches and set the charcoal to burning.

Outside in the darkness, rain beat on the roof and streamed down the windowpanes, but as the charcoal turned red hot in the brazier, it threw out a surprising warmth in spite of the vast, high-ceilinged room about them.

Once Adria came out of her door and stared at them from the hallway, but before Vicki could call to her to join them, she returned to the cold solitude of her bedroom.

During the evening Dad left his work and came to watch the game for a while. He stood behind Vicki and helped her now and then with moves, since she was a novice. She smiled at him a little shyly, wanting to make up for previous cross words unfairly spoken. Before he went back to work, he rested a hand affectionately on her shoulder. Even Mrs. Byrne seemed friendly tonight, and she brought a sweater she was knitting for Ken and sat beyond the *mangal*, sharing its warmth without any critical looks at Vicki.

Chess was difficult, and Vicki soon discovered that it was not to be learned as quickly as checkers or Monopoly. But the variety of moves the men could make was fascinating, and it was lovely to go sweeping down the board with her queen to take Ken's bishop, though humiliating when Ken turned right around and took her queen with a castle.

Even though Vicki was easily beaten, it was a long game—long because of the waits between plays when Ken would study the board and figure out what to do. It was during these waits that Vicki began to think about Adria. How lonely to be shut away from warmth and human company on this cold, rainy night. Adria must think they didn't want her with them.

When her king was finally checkmated and the game over, Vicki slipped away from the others and went down the hall to Adria's room. This part of the house seemed chill after the bright warmth of a glowing charcoal fire. She knocked softly on the door, and then more loudly when there was no answer.

"Who is it?" Adria called after the second knock.

"It's Vicki," she said. "Don't you want to come out for a while?"

There was a moment's silence before Adria answered. Then her words came coolly from beyond the closed door.

"I'm in bed," she said. "I'm reading. My story is interesting, and I don't want to get up."

"I—missed you," Vicki said softly. But there was no answer, and she went away from the door.

It was growing late, even for Saturday night, and before long the young people went to bed. Vicki undressed hurriedly in her chilly room, glad to crawl beneath the covers.

She hoped it wouldn't rain tomorrow when Meral Kirdar was coming.

She did not fall asleep at once—there were too many things to think about: Adria and the visit to Leyla and her grandparents, the way she had misjudged her father, Ken and the fact that he was turning out to be nice after all, in spite of his teasing. She thought about Mother at home too and was stirred by a longing for her. It was hard waiting for mail to come. Such a long way, even by air. And she thought about Adria again—because Adria was like the eye of a hurricane. The stormy winds of disaster whirled around her, and she stood there in the center defying everyone, following some strange storm pattern of her own. What was she up to? What dangerous, secret plan was she working on? And why did she, Victoria Stewart, have this curious feeling that she wanted to save Adria from hurt, save her from herself?

Finally, her own problems rose to engulf her, and once more her failure in school took its properly important place in her thoughts. In these late night hours, lying awake in the dark, a strange charity of vision came to her. A clarity that watching Adria had made possible. It was as if she looked into a mirror and saw Vicki Stewart from outside, objectively, the way she could see Adria. What she glimpsed was far from flattering. The glass, clear as still water, showed her someone who had failed in school though she had not needed to. Someone who said rude things to her aunts and made herself thoroughly unpleasant. Someone who had come to Turkey only because it meant escape from facing her friends, escape from the results of her own mistakes. But she had not run away from herself. That was the one thing she could not do.

It was long past midnight by the time she fell into a restless, haunted sleep. Her dreams were disturbing, moving close to the nightmare stage. It was as if she were in some cold, frightening place, from which there was no escape. Her feet felt like ice and a cold, dreadful blackness shut her in. Round and round she turned, and there was no way out, but only endless rows of windows and closed doors. Suddenly she knew she was in the harem part of the house, but now Adria was not with her and all around in the darkness were ghosts from the long-ago past, whispering and pointing, disliking her because she was here in a place that belonged to them.

She *must* get out—she must wake up! She knew this was a nightmare, and she had only to open her eyes to be rid of it. But her eyes would not open, or if they were open it made no difference. She tried to run and stumbled, falling to her knees. The floor was bare and cold beneath her hands, beneath her slipperless feet. And though her eyes were surely open, the crushing darkness, the sounds of rain all around, the whispering within, were clear and real.

Suddenly she knew the truth. This was no dream. She *was* awake. She was here in the haremlik alone in the middle of the night, and something was moving there in the darkness near her.

It was horrible not to know which way the door lay, to be hopelessly lost in the dark, with only the pounding of her own heart for company. When something came close and touched her on the arm, she cried out. It was only a weak cry. She was too frightened and helpless to scream out loud. At once fingers closed about her wrist, and a voice whispered in her ear.

"Don't be frightened—it's only me, Adria. Come along, and I'll take you back to the other part of the house. You must have walked in here in your sleep, Victoria. Everything's all right now. Don't be frightened."

The voice was so gently soothing that she could hardly recognize it as Adria's. The hand that clasped her own was firm and comforting. Still bewildered, her teeth chattering from the convulsive shivers that shook her, she let Adria guide her to the door and into the other part of the house. There a night light burned in the hall, and she could see her way.

"You're absolutely freezing," Adria said. "Come along with me. My bed's big enough for two, and I've got a hot-water bottle for your feet."

Vicki was too shaken to do anything but what Adria told her. It was wonderful to be tucked into a bed that was still warm and welcoming. Adria got in on the other side, but she left the bed lamp burning.

"Do you think I should call your father?" she asked. "Or Mrs. Byrne?"

"N-n-no!" Vicki chattered. "I'll b-b-be all right."

Gradually the shivering stopped, and warmth enveloped her.

"Do you often walk in your sleep?" Adria asked.

"Not much since I was quite small," Vicki said. "How did you happen to hear me?"

"I couldn't sleep," Adria admitted. "My thoughts kept going round and round, and I lay here and listened to the rain and the house creaking the way it does at night. So I heard your door when it opened, and I heard somebody come down the hall. When the footsteps went on past my door, I got up and looked out in time to see you step through the harem door and close it behind you. I couldn't believe you wanted to be in there in the dark, when I knew you were scared the other time we went into those rooms. So I moved fast. It's a good thing I was there when you woke up."

It was indeed, Vicki thought. She was especially struck by Adria's kindness. How strange people were—full of so many contrary traits and actions! Herself no less than anyone else. It almost seemed that it never paid to make up your mind about anyone—not once and for all. She was growing drowsy now in this comfortable warmth, but there was something she wanted to ask Adria. A thought that had come unexpectedly into her mind.

"Do you suppose—if I worked very hard all summer—I could make up for falling behind in school?"

Adria propped herself on one elbow and looked at her. In the light from the bed lamp her eyes were gray green and shining.

"Of course you could!" she cried softly. "If only you would, Victoria. Ken and I have lots of schoolbooks, and we could help you. And your father's a teacher."

Again Vicki was filled with surprise at Adria. Until now she had thought Adria uninterested in any problems except her own. Now she seemed as excited about this idea as though the difficulty were hers.

Vicki yawned mightily, and Adria reached up to turn off the light. They didn't need it now. Vicki was nearly asleep when Adria whispered to her in the darkness.

"I've thought of a wonderful plan," she said. "I think I know what Leyla meant when she spoke of a very old garden on a steep hillside—a place with walls. Now I know where to look for the ninth stone."

# 13

# Within the Fortress

Sometime during the night it stopped raining. By the time the cocks began to crow, the donkeys to bray, the goats to bleat, the sky above the Bosporus had cleared and a bright gold-and-pink sunrise was flushing the east. Vicki would have liked to sleep late, but Adria was up and hungry for breakfast. Clearly this was going to be one of Adria's good days—which was fine, since Meral was coming.

Vicki got up sleepily and continued to yawn through breakfast. Fortunately the rain sounds had hidden her sleepwalking, and no one else knew what had happened last night. Adria wouldn't tell, and Vicki had no desire to let her father know that she had gone back to infant ways, especially when this idea of making up her schoolwork had begun to seem attractive. True, it was not a new idea. Aunt May had tried to suggest such a plan, but Vicki had crossly brushed her aside. She was not sure exactly why, except that her own contrariness had been hard to fight. In fact, she had wanted to be contrary. Now it seemed easier to make up the work than to remain indignant with her teachers, her aunts, and even her father.

It would be nice if she could convince Adria that she too might profit by taking a new look at her problems. But Adria seemed so cheerful and happy this morning that Vicki had no desire to bring up the subject of the gold pin and spoil everything. With daylight, Adria seemed to have put out of her mind whatever notions she'd had about Leyla's spells and those nine stones.

130

Sunday morning they all went to a nearby church together, though in separate cars. Adria was happy to
come with Vicki and her father. Except for getting unbearably sleepy once or twice during the service, Vicki
found the experience a comforting one. There was serious
help for which she needed to ask, and the quiet of church
was the right place.

After church they drove home to a leisurely Sunday
dinner. When she had eaten, Vicki found herself sleepier
than ever. Fortunately, Meral's arrival helped to wake her
up. The Kirdars left their car and came in for a few moments. Meral's mother was young and quite beautiful. She
had the huge, dark eyes so many Turkish women did, and
she was dressed elegantly in the latest fashion. Her father
was tall and very handsome, and so was Meral's older
brother. But only Meral spoke English fluently, and the
others did not stay very long. They were driving on for
their visit in Bebek, and Nursel *hanimefendi*, as Adria
called Mrs. Kirdar, set a time when they would return for
Meral. When they'd gone, Vicki asked about the name
Adria had used.

"Nursel is her first name," Adria explained. "And *hanimefendi* is an especially courteous title. Until recently people used only first names in Turkey. Even now that the
Western custom of last names is accepted, first names are
still used most."

Mrs. Byrne was away for the afternoon, Ken was off
taking pictures, and Dad had an appointment across the
Bosporus. So the house was empty except for the three
girls and the servants.

After the Kirdars had left, Vicki invited Adria and
Meral up to her big room. Today the chill was gone, and
she could throw open the shutters on the veranda and let
in the sun. For a time Adria and Meral talked about
school, and Vicki tried to keep awake and listen. It was
easier when Adria got her recorder and played some
snatches from *Pinafore* while Meral sang. In spite of
seeming good in her part, Meral was still anxious and uncertain about her ability to carry off her role in an actual

performance. The time was not far off, and as it approached, she grew increasingly nervous.

During the afternoon, Meral noted a castle picture that Vicki had pasted to cardboard and set up on her dresser. This led Vicki to bring out the whole collection, and the girls spent considerable time poring over it.

"I have a picture I will give to you for this collection," Meral said. Today she was out of school uniform and looked very attractive in a yellow dress that reminded Vicki of sunlight.

"Of Rumeli Hisar?" asked Adria.

Meral shook her head with its thick crown of short dark hair. "No, this is a picture of the palace of my great-grandmother. We have several copies of the way it used to be."

You mean your great-grandmother owned a palace?" Vicki demanded, waking up.

"I do not say this correctly," Meral admitted and explained further. "It is not the palace of my great-grandmother but palace of sultan's sister. Not far from here on Bosporus. Very beautiful white palace with large pool. My great-grandmother has been lady-in-waiting to sultan's sister."

"How exciting!" Adria said. "It was considered a special honor to be in a palace household, wasn't it? Is the palace still there, Meral?"

"Road now cuts through where palace is," Meral said and waved her fingers as if causing the palace to vanish. "But place remains. Sometime I will show to you. You have seen Rumeli Hisar?" she added to Vicki.

"No, I haven't," Vicki said. "I've been waiting for someone to go there with me."

Adria jumped to her feet, and there was a sudden electric excitement about her. "Let's go now. It's a perfect time. Your parents won't mind, will they, Meral?"

"But, of course, they do not mind," Meral said, and she too seemed pleased with the idea: "I will tell to you Turkish history if we go now. Is most interesting place."

Though the day was sunny, the wind had a nip to it, so they got into light coats before going outside. Vicki found herself watching Adria uneasily. She did not like this sudden spurt of excitement. What was it Leyla had said—something about an ancient garden with walls going up a hill? In sudden conviction she knew that it was in Rumeli Hisar that Adria had thought of looking for her nine stones. There was nothing to do now but let her try. Sooner or later Adria would have to get this foolish search for a "golden horn" out of her system.

By the time they left, everyone was gone from the house. Adria said she would leave word with the Turkish maid, Fatma, as to where they would be, and they set off together down the winding road that led around the fortress.

From the level of the motor road edging the Bosporus, the stone walls and towers of Rumeli Hisar rose formidably stern and high. There was a ticket gate at the entrance, and Adria paid the small entrance fee for them all. They went through a deep, arching stone doorway onto a paved stone path within the fortress garden. This being Sunday, others were there as well, moving about the great expanse without crowding it.

The sight inside was surprising, and Vicki stood staring about in delight. All around the great garden ran high castellated walls, forming the outer lines of a triangle. It was a steep, irregular triangle, and at each point rose a high tower, very big around, commanding the waters of the Bosporus for miles. Smaller towers appeared here and there on the battlements and everywhere there were walks and steps along the high walls, following from tower to tower. Though the great stones from which all this was built were a mixture of black and dark gray, the towers had a warm, honey-bright look in the sunlight. The most surprising thing of all was the steep pitch of the hillside within the triangle. From the lowest tower close to the water, the interior fanned out and up almost vertically to the two highest towers far up the hill.

All the open space between had been shaped into grassy lawns and cobbled walks that zigzagged back and forth, connected with one another by steep flights of stone steps. All shrubbery had been cleared away, but here and there small trees stirred in the breeze and offered patches of shade. There were no buildings except for a strange central column of stone broken off some twenty feet in the air.

"What's that?" Vicki asked, looking up at the broken column partway up the hill.

"Once it was a minaret," Adria answered. "When the fortress was in use there was a small mosque for the soldiers. Am I right, Meral?"

"But, of course. You can see paved circle where mosque stood," said Meral.

Vicki threw Adria a quick look. Where, in a place as big as this and built from thousands of stones, did she think of searching for the nine stones Leyla had mentioned? But Adria did not seem discouraged. She was studying the higher walls, studying the levels all the way up.

"If it's here for me to find, it will speak to me," she said mystically.

Meral did not seem surprised by such a remark. "What is it that speaks to you?" she asked.

Before Vicki could distract her, Adria was pouring out the gypsy story. As they followed the walk beside the lower wall, she told of how Leyla had seen a golden horn in her hand last year and had found the same mark in Vicki's palm too and how the finding of the symbol would solve everything for Adria.

Vicki could not tell whether Meral was impressed or amused.

"You believe this?" the Turkish girl asked in a matter-of-fact tone.

Adria faced her honestly. "I don't know whether I do or not. I only know that I have to try every way I can to find out what she means."

"And if you do not find this—golden horn?" Meral asked.

Adria tilted her bright head, and a defiant smile touched her mouth. "I shan't depend on spells alone to help me. I know another way. A harder way, but I think it will work."

The dangerous excitement was upon her again, and Vicki's concern increased.

"What is it that you want so much?" Vicki asked.

Adria only laughed and ran ahead on the path, darting up a steep flight of steps to the next level of the hillside garden. High above, where it was too steep to mow, Queen Anne's lace, red poppies, and other small wild flowers grew in profusion. Vicki found herself looking from the pleasant slope of wild flowers to the high tower toward which Adria seemed to be climbing. The steps were steep and narrow up there at the top, and there were no railings to guard them. Along the top wall, the battlements offered protection, rising on one side, but the other side lay open, so that a misstep would mean a dangerous plunge.

Accustomed as she was to American safety measures in public places, Vicki considered the high walks in dismay. "Do they let people go up to the very top?"

"Why not?" said Adria. "I've been up there before with my father. The walks are wider than they look from here. You're perfectly all right if you keep to the inside and don't look down."

Vicki had no desire to trust herself not to look down, and she was glad when Meral objected to going any higher.

"Is not necessary to climb," she assured Vicki. "There is elevator in main tower. Very fine view from top."

"Let's go that way," Vicki said, ready to turn back and follow Meral's suggestion.

Adria did not remove her gaze from the heights. "Why don't you and Meral go up in the elevator in the main tower, while I climb to the high wall. I want to see if there's a place where I can count exactly nine stones."

The chouce was hard to make. Vicki had the feeling that she should not let Adria out of her sight, but at the same time she did not want to go scaling those unguarded heights.

Meral touched her arm lightly. "Come—I will show you the tower and tell to you about Rumeli Hisar. Adria is like a cat when she climbs. At school I have seen."

So it was settled, though Vicki still felt uneasy. Adria promised that she would come to the main tower when she was through. They could wait for her there. Up on the roof, if they liked.

On the way down, Vicki turned now and then to see Adria marching stanchly upward above them, her long, bright pony tail flying in the wind. Still higher, dwarfing her small figure rose the fearsome ramparts of the old fortress.

"More than five hundred years old," Meral said as they retraced their steps to the tower entrance. "Mohammed II said they must build to guard Bosporus and keep Constantinople safe from attack. He gives work to build each tower to three different viziers. Sultan Mohammed himself is in charge to build the walls. Many men go to work. Thousands. Fortress is finished in three months. My father says this is very difficult because of steep hill. See the cannon here beside the wall? Once these are set to guard towers and walls. Many soldiers come to live in the towers at this time. You will see old rooms when we go up."

"And did the fortress save the city?" Vicki asked as Meral led the way through a narrow, arched doorway in the base of the tower.

"No—Constantinople falls. For a time Rumeli Hisar is prison. But now is in good repair for all people to enjoy."

Inside the tower it was chilly and dim after the warm sunshine. The great interior walls were circular, following the shape of the tower, and a stone stairway wound about them, climbing around galleries toward the top. Off these galleries could be seen closed doors of the rooms that had once housed the garrison. There were more such rooms in the other towers as well, Meral said. Pigeons nested in the high ceiling of the tower, and their cooing sounds echoed eerily, magnified by the stone.

Meral and Vicki lined up with others to get into the elevator and were borne toward the roof. When they stepped out, they could look downward over the rail to the floor where they had recently stood. Not liking heights, Vicki drew back at once, and Meral led the way through a stone door and out onto a wide observation roof, floored in pale-red brick.

At once Vicki stepped to the wall on the inner side of the fortress and looked out upon the hillside. The view of marching walls and high towers was tremendous. But at the moment her attention focused upon the tiny figure of Adria, still climbing, her light dress easily seen against the dark gray of stone steps. Meral waved to her, but Adria was intent on her own affairs and did not look up to see them. After a moment of watching, the two girls went to the Bosporus side where they could enjoy the view.

"Over there is my village," Meral said, pointing. "Every day I come across by ferry. It is very close for my school."

They sat on a stone bench and talked for a while, and Vicki tried to put the nagging worry about Adria out of mind as she listened to Meral. The Turkish girl was critical, it seemed, of some of her friends at school.

"They are too silly," she said pleasantly, so that the word lacked the sharp sound it sometimes had when Vicki spoke it. "Some of my friends think only of clothes and games and marks in school. And of which teacher likes which girl best. Not all are like that but too many."

This did not sound very different from home, and Vicki said so. "American girls think of such things too. What do you think about, Meral?"

Meral's dark eyes seemed to glow with fervor. "Sometimes I think of my country. I think of how my mother's grandmother wore a veil and lived shut away in a palace where there are only women. But because of what Ataturk does for us, women now can be of use to Turkey. In very famous speech, Kemal Ataturk spoke to us who are living now."

The tower was empty of viewers for the moment, and Meral jumped up and struck a dramatic pose, as though she addressed a multitude. Vicki half expected her to twirl the imaginary mustache of the *Pinafore*'s captain. But as she began to speak, Vicki forgot her impulse to laugh. The Turkish girl was moved by a very real emotion as she repeated Ataturk's works.

" 'O Turkish child of future generations, it is your duty to save the independence, the Turkish Republic!' " she said dramatically, and then dropped to the bench and spoke earnestly to Vicki. "Those are words he says for all Turkish children to come. I must listen: I must help."

"But what can you do, Meral?"

"Perhaps I will be writer when I am grown. Perhaps for newspaper. Or perhaps I work on radio. I do not know. It is still hard for women in Turkey. But we are so small a country—all our people must work to keep freedom safe. That is why we like America. We have good friend in your country. Friend who believes like us in freedom. Russia is close—only across the Black Sea. And Russia does not like Turkey to be free."

Something of Meral's own feeling touched Vicki. "I'm glad I know you," she said warmly. "When I think of Turkey I'll always remember you here in Rumeli Hisar speaking those words."

There were tears of emotion in Meral's eyes when she looked at Vicki. However, since there was nothing either girl could do for Turkey at that moment, they descended from this high emotional plane and went over to the wall to see what Adria was doing. Though they searched the hillside from level to level, studying all those who moved upon steps or battlements, they could not see Adria anywhere.

"Perhaps she is inside high tower," Meral said. "I think she will come out soon."

They returned to watching boats upon the Bosporus and cars upon the road below. After a time, Meral stole a look at her watch. The afternoon was flying.

"Soon I must go to meet my mother and father," she said.

Once more Vicki searched steps and walks and hillside for some glimpse of Adria.

"I wonder if she could have fallen," she murmured aloud.

"Do not worry. She will come," Meral said.

But Vicki could not help worrying and Meral was aware of it.

"If you wish to stay, I can go back to house alone. Is not necessary for you to accompany me."

"I can't let you do that," Vicki said. "You're our guest. It would be terribly bad manners." Yet she hated the thought of leaving this place without Adria, of not being where Adria expected to find her.

"I understand," Meral said gently. "Adria is different. You must wait. I will explain. In such case is not bad manners."

Vicki thought Adria was being careless and inconsiderate. Perhaps the best thing to do would be to go home with Meral and forget about her. But she could not bring herself to do that. A horrid picture kept recurring in her mind—a vision of Adria lying at the foot of tower steps, alone and hurt. Last night Adria had come to her in the frightening world of the haremlik. She had been kind and thoughtful then. It would not be right to go away and leave her now.

Since Meral understood, Vicki went to the elevator with her and watched the car descend. After she had gone, Vicki went through another rather low doorway that opened off the circling gallery and found herself in a secluded, sunny embrasure where she could look down between the ramparts and watch the hillside. There was still no Adria in sight. The sleepiness that had threatened her all day long returned with several large yawns.

If she had to wait, she might as well be comfortable. Tucking her coat around her, she sat down with her back against a stone wall—and without intending to at all, fell fast asleep.

# 14

# On the Ramparts

Vicki wakened to a cold, cramped feeling. When she moved her arms and legs she found them stiff and was surprised to discover hard stone beneath her. Where could she be and why was it so dark? Surely she hadn't walked in her sleep again and wandered into the harem rooms of the house.

Almost at once she remembered and jumped up in concern. It was night. There were actually stars out overhead. She must have napped for ages. The utter quiet all about her was alarming. She felt her way to the parapet and looked down into the yawning triangle of the fortress garden. White walks and steps could be traced in the starlight, but lawns and trees were lost in shadow. The towers rode forbidding against the sky.

No one stirred in the enclosure, no one at all. The creaking of the elevator had ceased, the Sunday visitors were gone. Between Vicki and the outside gate stood the entire dark mass of the lower tower, with stairs circling down into blackness. She knew what it would be like in there without looking. She could not bear to step through the door into that dark and echoing tower. But neither could she stay here, shut into the fortesss of Rumeli Hisar all night long.

Surely that would not happen. Probably Adria had come to the roof to meet her and Meral. She might not have noticed this embrasure, only searching the main roof. Not finding them there, she would believe they had left. And she would have gone home herself. Then, surely,

140

when she found that Vicki was not there, she would come back here to look for her. Or at least, Adria would tell Dad where she was. Besides, they had left word with Fatma—she would tell them, even if Adria was late in coming. Only a light supper of soup and sandwiches had been planned for tonight, with no special time set for eating, since everyone would be returning at odd hours. Thinking of supper made her hungry and all the more uncomfortable.

She could not wait here to find out what was happening at home. Perhaps there were guards at the gate who stayed all night at the fortress. She leaned upon the parapet and called out as loudly as she could. At the first try her voice wavered. She called again, and the sound seemed to drift out into the great open space below and vanish—a thin, faint cry that no one would hear.

"It's no use," said Adria's voice behind her. "There's no one down there."

Vicki whirled about. She could just make out Adria's light dress slowing beneath her coat as she emerged from the dark doorway of the tower. All in one breath Vicki was startled and relieved and angry.

"Do you mean they've gone away and locked us in?" she cried. "Why didn't you wake me up? Why did you let me sleep if you knew I was here?"

There was a ringing sound of triumph in Adria's laughter, as though she knew that no one would hear her—and was glad of it.

"You looked so tired. I couldn't bear to wake you up. After all, you lost a lot of sleep last night."

"That's silly," Vicki said. "Now what are we to do? We've got to get out of this place. We can't stay here all night!"

"I don't suppose we'll have to," Adria said. "Sooner or later someone will get home and start looking for us."

"The maid will tell them," Vicki said.

In the pale starlight she could see Adria shaking her head in denial. "She won't tell them because she doesn't know. I only pretended I would let her know where we were going. You were fooled, weren't you, Victoria?"

Alarmed, Vicki turned and edged around the small space until she could look out toward the Bosporus. Lights climbed the hills on the Anatolia side and were reflected in dark water. The lights of a passing ship on its way to the Black Sea could be seen. Below the base of the fortress wound the motor road, with cars flicking past. The wind carried a whiff of exhaust fumes. Again Vicki tried to call out for help, and once more Adria stopped her.

"What's the use of scaring yourself by yelling like that? No one can hear you down there with cars going by. Besides, if we wait long enough, we'll be missed. Then Cousin Janet or your father will telephone Meral's parents, and Meral will say we were here. A search party will come down and look for us."

"And in the meantime we'll have to wait in this awful place," Vicki protested.

A fiercer gust of a wind that must be blowing straight from the Black Sea cut across their portion of roof, and Vicki turned up her coat collar. This was much colder than last night.

Adria was silent, and Vicki peered at the hazy outline of her face. Anger was growing inside her and bewilderment too.

"Everyone will be worried about us. Don't you care?" she asked. "Don't you mind playing an unkind trick like this? Why should you want to do it?"

"I don't want to," Adria said surprisingly. "I hate it— the way I hated that trick I played on Ken. But it's the only way. Come along. Let's get out of this tower at least."

There was no figuring out what Adria meant, but Vicki was sure about one thing.

"If you think I'm goind down those stairs in pitch darkness, you're crazy. In fact, I think you're a little crazy anyway."

"Don't be so silly," Adria said impatiently. "I've brought a flashlight. We won't have any trouble."

"You—you brought a flashlight?" Vicki stammered. "You mean you planned this all along?"

Adria switched on the beam of light and disappeared through the door. Her voice drifted back, echoing a little from the interior of the tower.

"Of course I planned it. I had the flashlight in my coat pocket all the time. Though I didn't know you were going to go to sleep and be here with me. I meant to stay out of sight until everyone was gone. Then the uproar would concern only me. I knew about this little corner, and I came right here because it was a good place to hide while people were leaving. When I found you asleep, I waited."

Vicki went through the low opening to stand beside Adria in the darkness of the top gallery. The flashlight beam looked as tiny as a candle up here. All the rest of the tower was like a well of black fog. It smelled cold and damp and tinged with the unknown. She did not want to argue with Adria now. But she wanted to get out of this place.

Adria reached for her hand, and they began the long descent, following close to the curve of the wall. Around and around. Down long flights of steps and around a gallery and down again. Overhead the pigeons, disturbed in their sleep, made soft sounds in the darkness. Once Vicki's foot struck a pebble, and it went flying off into space. It seemed an age before it struck the stone floor far below. If ever she got out of this experience alive, Vicki thought, she would tell Adria exactly what she thought of her and her ridiculous plans.

Step by step, following the small circle of light, they went down, and eventually the bottom was reached.

"There," said Adria, "that wasn't so bad, was it?"

They walked out into the brighter triangle of the fortress garden, and in this low place, sheltered by the wall, the wind did not reach them. Crickets were chirping in the grass, and beyond the wall cars whooshed by indifferently. From the water came the mournful wail of a boat whistle.

Adria spread her arms wide. "What a beautiful, clear night! What a wonderful place to be! Now I can go to the very top and search a while longer. With no people around to wonder what I am doing."

Vicki allowed her exasperation to sound in her voice.

"Do you mean you played a trick like this because of a lot of foolish fortunetelling?"

"No," said Adria, "I didn't. But now that I have the opportunity I'm not going to miss it. You can come or not as you like." And she started up a zigzag path that led along the hill.

It would be worse to be left alone than to follow Adria, so Vicki hurried after her. Besides, she still meant to say what she thought of this harebrained escapade, if only Adria would stop to listen. It was as difficult to tell her anything as it would be to hold a handful of starlight in your fingers. Adria was like that—drifting away even as you reached out to touch her or scold her.

Up they went, with Adria choosing the shortest, steepest way, climbing until all the safe open paths of the garden were below them and only steep, unguarded castle steps lay ahead.

"Wait!" Vicki called. "Do we have to go any higher?"

"I do," Adria said. "But I'm willing to stop and rest awhile. Let's sit on the steps. Don't be so angry with me, Victoria. Just live what's happening now. Such a beautiful night and such a strange, wonderful place! Ever since Leyla told me she'd once spent a night in here, I've wished it could happen to me. And now it has."

"Maybe you're going to spend a night here, but I'm not," Vicki said, finding it impossible to appreciate her surroundings under the circumstances.

She sat on stone steps beside Adria and looked down at the black tower where they had been so recently, and at the broken column of the minaret, silvered with starlight on the open hillside.

Adria touched her arm lightly. "Look up—don't look down. Look up at all the fire-folk."

In spite of not wanting to do anything Adria suggested, Vicki stared up at the sky with all its millions and billions of stars. How bright they were, seen from this dark place with no city lights to dim their brilliance.

"Do you know the words?" Adria asked softly. "I can remember my mother reading the verses aloud to me. Let's see if I can say them—

" 'Look at the stars! look, look up at the skies!
  O look at all the fire-folk sitting in the air
  The bright boroughs, the circle-citadels there!' "

The two on the hillside were quiet, watching the stars, and something of Vicki's anger began to subside. In so many ways, Adria was appealing and rather touching. In spite of trouble to come, Vicki knew she would remember this moment all her life. On bright nights in later years when she looked up at the skies she would see again the fire-folk above this strange Turkish hillside.

"I don't remember the rest," Adria said, "but there's another line I like.

" 'The gray lawns cold where gold,
    where quickgold lies!' "

Again the words were as much to be felt as to be heard, and the gray lawns of Rumeli Hisar seemed to shine with quickgold beneath the stars. But Vicki could not sit here dreaming forever under Adria's strange spell that was as magic as anything Leyla could weave. At least, when Vicki spoke, it was more gently than before.

"I don't understand anything about you, Adria. Don't you mind at all that your Cousin Janet and my father will be worried about us? Don't you mind how angry they are going to be?"

Adria turned to her earnestly. "I won't let them be angry with you, Victoria. I won't let you be blamed this time. The fault is all mine—every bit of it. And I'll tell them so."

"I don't know what's going to happen," Vicki said, not in the least reassured.

"I do!" said Adria. "The thing I've been trying to make happen is sure to happen now. Cousin Janet isn't happy about taking me back to the States with her. I've been giving her nothing but trouble, and she knows Ken doesn't like me. I only wish he had told her about our running away from him in the bazaars yesterday. And about what I did to his tools."

"How can you be so mean?" Vicki asked. "You don't seem like a mean person. Sometimes you're very kind and considerate."

Adria clenched her hands upon her knees. "Maybe it's harder than you think. But I must be mean, I must! Tonight will finish what I've started. Cousin Janet will say she's had enough and that she won't take me home with her for anything."

So this was the goal Adria had been striving for with all her tricks!

"And then what?" Vicki asked.

"Then I can stay in Turkey." Adria opened her arms again, held them wide, encompassing Rumeli Hisar and all the land outside, the very Bosporus beyond. "This is my home. I've only visited America once. I don't really know America, any more than you know Turkey."

Vicki could understand Adria's plan clearly enough, but she could see no solution.

"How can you stay here?" she asked. "Who would you stay with? You'd have to live with someone related to you. Who else is there?"

With a quick gesture, Adria pulled off the fastening that held her hair in a pony tail, and let it blow free about her shoulders, as if the gesture might free her thoughts from earthbound ways.

"I don't know," she said. "There *has* to be a way. I'm sure that's what Leyla was promising me when she told my fortune. If only I knew what the golden horn was, I'd know how I could stay in Turkey. Don't you see, Victoria—I can still feel my father and mother in these places where I've been with them. There are so many people here who knew them. If I had to give up and go away, it would be like—like shutting a door on everything that has been wonderful and important in my life. It would be like forgetting them. I can't do that."

Vicki sat very still, and there was an aching in her for Adria. The girl beside her was weeping softly now. There must be something to say that would comfort her, that would give her some sort of hope. But Vicki did not feel old enough or wise enough to meet so difficult a problem.

For a little while she let Adria cry and when she spoke her words came haltingly, for she was very uncertain.

"I don't think answers to troubles lie in—in spells, Adria. I think they lie in people. Not in other people—in us. Maybe when a door shuts that isn't going to open again, we have to go on from there. We can't go back. Not ever. So it's what happens now that counts. I can't go back to where I was before either. I have to go on from where I am now."

To her surprise Adria leaned over and set a quick, light kiss on her cheek. "I *do* like you, Victoria. You're so sensible that you almost hold me down to earth. Almost, but not quite." She sprang up, her hair flying. "Come along—let's go to the top. It's up there I want to count the stones."

Vicki tried to resist. "I hate high places. I don't want to go up there."

"I'll hold onto you," said Adria. "Besides—" she paused as if thinking up some new idea, "—besides, once we're up on the wall we can see down into the road that leads uphill to our house. Perhaps someone will come along it, and we can call for help."

Adria would go up there anyway, Vicki knew, and it was better to make the climb than to be left alone on this lower level.

She clung to Adria's hand and was glad that it wasn't light enough for her to see how far she might fall if she made a misstep. Toward the top the steps grew narrow. Looking always up and never down, Vicki hugged the wall behind Adria and put her feet down firmly, until at last they came out upon a level walk that ran along the highest ramparts of the fortress. Here the outer wall rose beside them, and they could look down through a space in the battlements to the faint curving line of road where it wound up the hill. A road completely empty—with not a donkey or a goat or a person moving on its whole shadowly length.

Adria threw the beam of her flashlight along the battlements and tried all sorts of counting combinations without arriving at the magic number of nine. Vicki paid little attention. She had no belief in Leyla's spells, and she found this high place terrifying.

She turned her back upon the descent and clung to the wall as if she thought it might move away from her. All her annoyance with Adria was sweeping back.

"I want to go down!" she cried. "I don't want to stay in this awful place one minute longer."

Abruptly Adria stopped counting and switched off her light. "All right. I don't think I'm going to find the right stone anyway. I'd rather wait till someone comes to look for us, but if you're frightened, we'll go home right away. Besides, I'm getting hungry."

"Right away?" Vicki echoed, trying to see Adria's face. "How can we go when we can't get out?"

Adria's laugh had a shivery sound there on the dim ramparts. "We walk through the gate, of course. Come along."

"But—but you said we were locked in and—"

"I didn't say we were locked in—you did," Adria told her. "The gate is open. I checked earlier. There's a guard who lives here all the time, but he's gone off for dinner, or to see his friends or something, and he left the gate open. After all, who would come in and steal the cannons?"

This further trick seemed the last straw, but Vicki put off her reproaches until later. All she wanted now was to be outside the forbidding walls of this Turkish fortress. When Adria moved toward the first flight of steps, Vicki followed her. But the steps were narrow and dark, and now she could see their steep downward pitch into space. In sudden terror, she shrank against the wall, frozen and unable to move.

"Do come along," Adria said. "Give me your hand. You'll be all right."

But Vicki knew she would not be all right. Going down would be much worse than coming up. Going down, she would have to look, and the very thought turned her to stone.

"I can't," she whispered. "I can't make it."

Adria looked at her anxiously. "Goodness—you are frightened. My mother used to be like that about high places. It's something you can't help, I suppose. If you're that frightened, we can't go down without someone who is strong enough to help you. That means we'll have to stay for now. I'm sorry, Victoria. I didn't know you'd feel like this."

Adria returned to the space between the battlements, and Vicki leaned beside her as she flashed her light, signaling to anyone who might see them down there on the road. But nothing moved, nothing happened. Above the fortress, a thin crescent moon had risen, shedding little more light on the scene than did the pale stars. It rode the sky serenely, with a single star close above it. Almost like the Turkish flag with its star and crescent, Vicki thought, staring up at the sky.

It was the sound of whistling that brought her attention back to earth. Someone down there on the road was walking toward the fortress and he was whistling "Yankee Doodle." She snatched the flashlight from Adria's hands and began to wave its beam madly back and forth.

"Ken!" she shouted. "Ken, we're up here on the wall!"

A second flashlight came on down in the road, and they could make out a dim figure looking up at them.

"Vicki?" he called. "Adria? What are you doing up there?"

Vicki waited for no complicated explanations from Adria. There was nothing wrong with her voice now. She spoke out good and strong, so that Ken could hear every word.

"Never mind how we got here. I can't climb down in the dark, and the guard isn't here. Get someone to come for us. Why didn't you look for us sooner?"

"I got home only a little while ago," he called back. "There was nobody there but the servants. Meral left a note thanking us for having her over, and explaining that she had to leave you in the fortress, Vicki, because Adria was lost. Mom and your dad were coming home as I left, so I put the note out for them and came running down here to see if I could raise anybody by shouting. Now I'll go back and start things going to get you out. Stay where you are until somebody comes with lanterns."

"We'll stay," Vicki promised fervently.

The flashlight vanished up the road, and she was so relieved she could have hugged Adria. But Adria was hugging herself. She had clasped her arms around her body in delight, and for a moment Vicki thought she was glad about getting out. She might have known better than to expect a sensible reaction from Adria.

"What a rumpus there's going to be!" Adria cried. "I can hardly wait to see Cousin Janet's face. There's going to be a real uproar. And it will be all my fault, every bit of it!"

"I certainly hope it will be," Vicki said, both disgusted and doubtful.

In the time they had to wait before the guard was located, she had a good deal of time to think. And the more she considered her story about staying behind, falling asleep, and being in here with Adria by sheer accident, the less convincing it sounded. She was not sure the whole fault would be considered Adria's by any means. And just when she had wanted *not* to have any more trouble. Just when she had thought about making up her studies and catching up in school so that she could redeem herself. Just when she and her father had begun to know each other a little better than had seemed possible in quite a while.

It appeared a longer time than it was before sound of rescue reached them and the welcome light of lanterns appeared down the hill by the gate. By the time Dad and the Turkish guard climbed up to bring them down, even Adria was no longer quite so cocksure as she had been of what would happen next.

# 15

# The Gypsy's Message

When she looked back on it later, the scene at the house that night was something Vicki wanted only to forget. To give Adria credit, she had gone through with her effort to exonerate Vicki from blame. But it was an effort far from successful.

After a quick supper, something of a trial had been held in the upstairs salon, with everyone present, including Ken. Dad had suggested that matters be left till morning, but Mrs. Byrne was too upset and angry, and Adria too anxious to let everyone know what she had done. So the whole story was poured forth without the least glossing over, and Vicki's own account of what had happened sounded as lame as she had expected it to.

Adria was in all the trouble she could ever hope to be, and before she was sent off to bed, Mrs. Byrne made an exasperated announcement.

"This can't go on," she said. "I will not have my household disrupted by the inconsiderate way in which you behave, Adria. You're too much for me. The first thing tomorrow morning I'm going to write to your Uncle Hinton Brace."

Adria's eyes widened in her white face. "Uncle Hinton? He won't care what happens to me. He never approved of Father. He was much older, and he doesn't like children. Besides, he travels all the time for his import business."

"Nevertheless," said Mrs. Byrne, "he is a closer relative to you than I am. I have done what I could. The responsibility is now his. We'll discuss it no further."

Adria jumped up and ran off to her room. Vicki was about to go mournfully away to her own room, when Mrs. Byrne spoke to her directly.

"I'm very sorry to see you involved in this escapade, Vicki. I would have thought you had enough to worry about."

Dad raised his eyebrows inquiringly, but Vicki said nothing and Mrs. Byrne did not push the matter further. Dad let her go with only a quiet "Good night," and tears were stinging her eyelids as she hurried to her room.

Only Ken came after her. "Can't you stay away from Adria?" he asked. "Don't you know by now that she's poison?"

Vicki blinked to keep from disgracing herself further and went quickly into her room and shut the door. Ken meant to be sympathetic, but she didn't want his sympathy right now.

The castle pictures were still strewn about where she had left them after showing them to Meral, and she sighed. She would never have guessed that what had seemed an innocent visit to the fortress would turn out so badly. She did not think she would ever want a picture of Rumeli Hisar for her collection.

Nevertheless, she was tired enough to sleep well and long that night. She did not waken until morning, when she heard Adria's secret scratching signal at the door. At first she did not answer, pretending to be asleep. But Adria was persistent, and she did not wait for Vicki's answer but opened the door herself and came over to the bed.

"You're awake, aren't you?" she said. "Though I don't blame you if you don't want to talk to me."

Vicki opened her eyes and stared at the other girl. Adria was dressed in her school uniform, and her hair was neatly braided so that she did not look like a flyaway nymph this morning. Her cheeks seemed a little puffy, and there was a redness about her eyes that meant she had been crying.

"Uncle Hinton is a dreadful person," she said despairingly. "He's horribly strict and stodgy. He never liked

Dad's being an artist, and he used to tell Mother he was sorry for her. Sorry for a person like Mother, who was always so contented and happy! Once I heard him say that I was too much like my father for my own good. What am I going to do, Victoria?"

Vicki propped herself up in bed and yawned widely. "Maybe you could start thinking things out ahead of time before you fly into such complications," she said, sounding cross and impatient to her own ears and not caring a bit. Adria deserved whatever she was getting.

Adria did not take offense. "I don't blame you for being angry. They wouldn't believe me last night when I told them none of this was your fault. So now I've got you in wrong too."

"What else could you expect?" Vicki snapped. "Oh, Adria, why don't you grow up? Nine stones! Lines in your hand! Golden horns and gypsy fortunetelling! And trying to make people mad, of all things! What do you think can happen except more trouble?"

To her surprise, Adria's eyes actually brightened. "Of course! After all that happened last night, I'd forgotten. Now I must find the golden horn, whatever it is. I must see Leyla again—that's the only possible way out that's left for me."

The trouble with Adria, Vicki thought, was that she kept mixing up real things with make-believe. Children did that when they were small, but as you grew up you had to figure out which was which and keep the two separated. There seemed to be no way to make Adria understand this.

"I know only one thing," she told the other girl. "You've got to behave like an angel from now on. That's your only chance if you want to change your Cousin Janet's mind. If having Uncle Hinton for your guardian is worse than having Mrs. Byrne, then you'd better turn over a new leaf."

"I don't want either of them—" Adria began, but Vicki broke in at once.

"You don't have any other choice, do you? Right now I

wish you'd get busy and help me find Mrs. Byrne's pin so I could get out of my troubles."

Adria looked stricken. "How awful! I forgot you were still being blamed for that. Of course I'll have to tell her the truth right away."

"And make sure she'll turn you over to Uncle Hinton?" Vicki asked impatiently. "That will be fine, won't it?"

At her words, Adria looked so forlorn and discouraged, and Vicki's heart softened.

"Will you do as I say and behave from now on?" Vicki asked. "You can't change what's done. That's another closed door. But maybe there are new doors to open, if you'd only try."

"All right," Adria agreed. "I'll try. I'll try with all my heart. I'll be so good and thoughtful and—"

"Try to be yourself," said Vicki. "You could be an awfully nice person if you wouldn't think up such wild schemes. You were *trying* to get into trouble, remember? Now you have. And maybe it's harder to get out than in."

"Do dress and come down to breakfast with me," Adria pleaded. "I don't want to face Cousin Janet alone."

Vicki agreed and when she was ready, they went downstairs together, to find the others already eating. It was a restrained meal, with Dad and Mrs. Byrne keeping up the conversation as if they were deliberately avoiding unpleasant topics. No reference was made to last night, and Adria was very quiet and polite, quick to pass the cream and sugar and say, "Yes, sir," and "No, ma'am." Vicki could only hope that she was as chastened as she seemed.

Not until the meal was nearly over and Dad was about ready to drive to school, did Mrs. Byrne suddenly remember something.

"I'm sorry," she said to Adria. "I had a message for you, but what with all that has happened, I completely forgot to give it to you. It was from that gypsy girl—what was her name?"

"Leyla?" Adria asked, and Vicki's interest quickened.

Mrs. Byrne nodded. "When I drove down to the Galata area yesterday to inquire about boat trips up the Bosporus, she was there. She saw me when I left the car and came running over to speak to me. She seemed terribly upset. In fact, she was crying so hard I could hardly understand what she was saying. It seems that her little sister is missing and—"

"Oh, not Cemile!" Adria cried.

Vicki listened in distress as Mrs. Byrne went on.

"Yes—the little sister. I couldn't make out the details—Leyla was too excited for her English to be very good."

"That's awful," Adria said. "Cemile is all Leyla has. I'm very fond of her. I'd like to go to her grandparents' house to see her, if I can."

"You wouldn't be in time to catch her," Mrs. Byrne said. "Leyla told me she was only staying in Istanbul for her sister's sake. Now she's going back to her people to see whether the child went there. She's leaving Istanbul today. She wanted to see you, but there would be no time because you'd be in school, so she gave me a rather strange message for you."

Perhaps it would be better for them all if Leyla went away, Vicki thought. Then Adria could forget about her. Forget about fortunetelling. But it was unbearably sad about poor little Cemile, and there was no way for Adria to help.

Mrs. Byrne was trying to remember the message. "I'm not sure I've got it right. The girl said something about a palace garden near Bebek. She didn't have the right word, but she made gestures in the air to make what I think meant three levels up. And then she said 'nine stone,' quite clearly and motioned to the right. I hope it makes sense to you, Adria. It doesn't mean anything at all to me."

"Thank you for telling me," Adria said. "I—I'll try to figure it out. I'm sorry I won't be able to see her. I hope Cemile has gone to the gypsy camp."

It was getting late, and Dad signaled that they would have to be on their way. The two girls had a moment alone while Dad was getting out the car.

"What do you think Leyla meant?" Adria pondered. "There isn't any palace near Bebek. While Rumeli Hisar might be called a castle, it's not a palace at all. I feel more mixed up then ever."

"Don't think about it," Vicki urged. But she knew that Adria would probably do little else than think about it from now on. And about what might have happened to Cemile.

Dad honked the horn, and Adria hurried away, leaving Vicki to face the long day ahead by herself.

She went up to her room, feeling gloomy, both about Cemile and Adria, and about the muddle her own affairs were in. Under such circumstances she felt hesitant about bringing up a plan for making up her schoolwork. If she mentioned it now, everyone would think she was trying to make up for a guilty conscience. She couldn't blame Dad, or even Mrs. Byrne, for what they thought of her. How it looked to them was perfectly clear. But neither could she do as Ken advised and regard Adria as poison, push her away, refuse to help. Adria would tell the truth about the pin if she urged her to. But Vicki knew she could not. Adria's troubles were worse than her own.

In the end, she sat down and wrote a very long letter to her mother. She did her best to tell about everything exactly as it had happened. She tried to make it clear that Adria would be a fine person if only she gave herself a chance. To her mother she could write as well about her own resolve to make up her schoolwork—or at least to try as hard as she could.

When the letter was finished, written small on thin paper, and sealed in an airmail envelope, she felt a little better. Everyone needed someone to talk to and at home the aunts had kept telling her not to worry Mother. But if she knew anything about her mother, this letter would help matters, not make them worse. Writing it had helped. Adria had no one to whom she could talk. No one older and wiser. She had only Victoria Stewart.

A few days later, a letter from her mother arrived. Not in answer to hers, of course—it was too soon for that. Mother wrote cheerfully, telling about amusing things at the hospital and about how the aunts had got safely off on their ship for a trip around the world.

"I'm glad you went to Turkey cheerfully, Vicki dear," she wrote, and Vicki found her ears burning a little at the thought of how uncheerfully she had gone. "It helped me a lot to know that you'd be with Dad and everything would be fine for you."

So no one had told her about her daughter's failure in school, Vicki thought. Now that letter would come filled with its story of woe. Still, she could not wholly regret writing it. She could almost hear Mother saying, "But that's what mothers are for."

The days before the performance of *Pinafore* was held at the school were surprisingly quiet and uneventful. Adria continued on her best behavior, and while Mrs. Byrne had not wholly relented, she'd said nothing more about the letter to Uncle Hinton, and there was no telling whether or not she had written it.

As far as Dad was concerned, Vicki found everything was still stiff and uncomfortable. He was absorbed in his research, and it was almost as though he had forgotten his daughter's presence. Perhaps he thought about her only when she got into trouble, she told herself in annoyance. But that wasn't fair, and she tried to dismiss the notion. The fact remained that they did not know each other very well and that their relationship was not improving.

# 16

# Stage Fright

The Music Club of the Orta Okul, or Prep School, was to hold its performance of excerpts from *H.M.S. Pinafore* during the last hour of the day, with girls from all classes invited, as well as whatever mothers wished to come. Vicki's invitation from Meral was now official, and on the afternoon of the appointed day, Mrs. Byrne drove her to the school and left her there.

Vicki knew her way through the grounds now, and she walked past the basketball and volleyball courts and found the school building without difficulty. A teacher in the corridor showed her the way to the assembly hall, and she went into the big room to discover that she was early. What Adria called the "Orta Okul Philharmonic" was rehearsing ahead of time.

Vicki slipped quietly into a seat and looked about with interest. At first glance, the room seemed like an assembly hall in one of the older schools back home. But there were certain differences. The balcony that ran across the back and along each side had an iron railing of Turkish design. Directly above the small stage that bulged into the room, and was outlined in red velvet draperies, hung a framed picture of the man whose face Vicki was coming to know—Mustafa Kemal—Ataturk.

A lively rendition of "Little Buttercup" was being played, and she sat back to listen. The "orchestra" was made up of six girls with recorders and the music teacher at the piano. Oddly enough, Adria was not among them—a fact that started a faint tugging of worry in

158

Vicki's mind. Before the piece was finished, the teacher broke off and waved her hands at the girls.

"No—no, you're blowing too hard. Blow softly, and you won't make that horrid sound."

The girls giggled and whispered, then put their recorders to their lips again. They looked so much like girls at home that Vicki felt homesick for a moment.

Other performers were running back and forth, more or less in costume, and a second teacher was helping. There was some concern about Little Buttercup, who looked very gay in white blouse and flowered skirt, with a lavender shawl about her shoulders and a pancake of straw hat on her head. Her make-up had been plastered on with a lavish hand, and the teacher shook her head despairingly.

"You do not like?" Buttercup said. "I can take off."

"It will make a mess if you take it off now, Nesrin," Miss Bronson said. "There's not time. Remember to speak your words carefully, and don't take up the whole stage."

Sir Joseph, by her accent clearly an American girl, came rushing out from backstage. Her naval officer's uniform, trimmed with what were undoubtedly her father's medals, and pulled in sack-fashion around the waist, was hung with a huge sword that clanked dramatically and threatened to get between her legs. She was not playing Sir Joseph at the moment, however.

"We can't find the captain anywhere," she told Miss Bronson. "Meral was in school—I saw her in class this morning. But she isn't here now."

"That's not like Meral—she's very dependable," Miss Bronson said. "Do look around for her, but don't stay away. You'll need to be onstage in fifteen minutes."

The orchestra members had paused to listen to this excitement, and one of them spoke up.

"Adria is not here too," she said.

"Yes, I know," the music teacher agreed. "But she's in school, and I've been expecting her to appear at any moment."

Meral and Adria both missing, Vicki thought. If it had been one or the other—but both together made it a real cause for worry. Had Adria pulled another trick so that Meral had found it necessary to go after her?

Without speaking to anyone, Vicki left her seat and found her way to the door of the school building. Once outside, she began to hurry.

Along a woodsy path she ran, following the way toward the place they called the Plateau. She was driven by a hunch—a hunch so strong that it would not be denied. Perhaps she was wrong, but if she was right . . .

By the time she left the woods and found the path around the field, she was out of breath. Her hunch was right! She could see them both now. Near the twisted tree Meral sat on a bench with her head bent, her face hidden in her hands. She was dressed in a white blouse and long navy-blue slacks, which were tucked into red rubber boots and belted in red leather—her captain's costume. Her dark hair had been parted in the middle and brushed into a style not unlike the way men had worn their hair long ago. Before her stood Adria, her recorder still in hand, apparently pleading excitedly with Meral.

As Vicki reached them, Adria looked around in relief. "Thank goodness you're here! Maybe you can talk to her. She's come down with a terrible state of stage fright and doesn't want to go back and play her part."

"What's the matter, Meral?" Vicki asked. "Everyone's waiting for you."

Meral took her hands from her face and looked up tragically. A charcoal mustache had been painted on her upper lip, a goatee on her chin, and her eyebrows had been given a stern twist with black pencil. Her expression, however, was not that of the *Pinafore*'s bold captain, but of a terrified girl.

"I cannot do it!" she wailed. "All the words are forgotten. The music I do not remember. All is gone. And my mother comes to see me. I am disgraced. I fail my teacher. She worked very hard to teach me, and now I do not remember anything."

"She's got it bad," Adria said. "What are we going to do?"

Somehow Vicki found herself taking charge. This was

something she understood. It was not like being caught on the heights of a fortress.

"You'd better hurry right back, Adira," she said. "You can't be in any more trouble yourself. Don't worry—I'll get Meral there in time. Tell them she'll be coming."

Adira gave her a look of gratitude and took a short cut, running across the grassy field. Vicki drew a deep breath and turned her attention to the emotion-shaken girl before her. She hoped she could sound more confident than she felt at the sight of her.

"Come along, Meral. There's still time. I'll walk back with you."

"I cannot walk," Meral wailed. "My knees do not wish to walk."

"Of course you can walk," Vicki said sternly. "You're being foolish, you know. It's much worse not to show up at all than to forget some of the words or sing off key. If you stay here, they can't put on the performance at all. The captain's role is too important to skip. That's why it was given to you. Because you do it so well, and they knew they could count on you."

Meral opened her mouth for another protest, but Vicki would not listen. She took her by the arm and pulled her to her feet.

"Hold on to me and we'll start back. It will be all right as soon as you're out on the stage—you'll see. I know. I've been every bit as scared as you are. In fact, I'm always scared when I'm in a play."

To her relief, Meral actually got up and began to walk with her. Vicki continued her earnest patter as they moved in the direction of the school.

"I found out something the last time I had stage fright. Being scared doesn't matter. The more worried you are ahead of time, the better you'll be. You don't need to struggle to remember the words. All you need to do now is bluff."

"Bluff?" Meral repeated blankly. "What is this—bluff?"

"You put on an act, Meral. You swagger the way the captain would swagger. You make faces and scowl. That's easy to do. And if you do it, nobody will suspect that you're scared. That's the secret—not letting anyone guess. All the rest will come easily. You'll hear the music, and the teacher will give you the words if you forget. You're going to be a wonderful captain, Meral. Your mother and your teachers and—and Turkey will be proud of you."

The picture of Turkey being proud of one young girl in a school performance of *Pinafore* was too much for Meral's excellent sense of humor. She began to laugh, and Vicki squeezed her arm encouragingly as they hurried toward the school.

"That's fine, Meral. When you see that something's funny, you can't be scared. But don't laugh like a girl— laugh like the captain of the *Pinafore*."

Meral's sudden roar of deep laughter startled the birds from the trees and made one of the gardeners turn around to stare. The girls began to run now and by the time they reached the others backstage, Meral was only a little late. The audience was already in place in the assembly hall, with the mothers sitting in the front rows.

Miss Bronson greeted Meral without question and hurried her into place behind the lowered curtain. Left alone, Vicki felt a bit limp. There wasn't much space backstage—just a small bare room at the foot of steps that led up to the stage. She looked at herself in a mirror hanging slightly askew from a nail in the wall and was surprised. The Vicki Stewart who stared back at her looked brightly interested in what was going on, and a flush of excitement touched her cheeks.

She returned to the hall with a small feeling of triumph that she did not want to suppress. She *was* good for something after all.

Adria, seated with the musicians, saw her and gestured toward the front seats as she went past. Meral's mother sat in the second row and when Nursel *hanimefendi* motioned to her to take the next seat, Vicki sank into it gratefully. It was good to sit down and catch her breath. Her worry wouldn't be over until she saw how Meral performed up there on the stage, but for now she had done all she could.

Mrs. Stone, the music teacher, struck a chord on the piano, the recorders began the opening notes, up went the curtain, and there was the cast onstage. In the back rows, standing on tiered steps, were the girls who played the sailor chorus. In front stood Little Buttercup, Josephine the captain's daughter, the captain swaggering and scowling, Sir Joseph manfully struggling with a very large sword, and Ralph Rackstraw the romantic hero, looking a bit too much like the very pretty Turkish girl who played the role.

Little Buttercup, her rouge somewhat subdued by the lights, straightened her lavender shawl and began to sing.

> "I'm called Little Buttercup—dear Little Buttercup,
>     Though I could never tell why . . ."

Meral, her arms folded, looked every bit the captain in command. When her turn came, she was a huge success, and Vicki was able at last to draw a deep breath of relief. Only one touch was wrong—the captain of the *Pinafore* wore clasped about one forearm a wide silver bracelet.

Near the end of the performance, when everyone gathered to sing the lovely song to the moon, it was very effective, and Vicki found herself humming the words under her breath.

> "Fair moon, to thee I sing,
>         Bright regent of the heavens;
>     Say, why is everything
>         Either at sixes or at sevens?"

When it was over, everyone crowded up to congratulate the cast. Meral, excited and laughing, came at once to tell her mother what had happened and how she had very nearly not appeared at all.

"It is Vicki who makes me to come," Meral said. "She tells to me that I must make a bluff—and this I do!" With a sudden gesture she unclasped her silver bracelet and snapped it about Vicki's arm. "Is for you," she said warmly. "For good friend from America. *Güle, güle*, wear it in healthy and happy days."

Vicki stared at the lovely silver band in surprise. "Oh, no—I couldn't—" she began.

"You must," Adria told her quickly. "It is a Turkish custom. You'd hurt Meral's feelings if you gave it back. Besides, she's right. You did save the day."

Nursel *hanimefendi* nodded her approval and pleasure. She spoke no English, but through Meral she expressed her gratitude and invited Vicki and Adria to come with them to tea.

When the American girls had let Mr. Stewart know they wouldn't be going home with him, they went to the Kirdars' car and drove along the Bosporus to a nearby open-air tea place. The car was parked, and they got out.

Arranged in rows on the gentle slope up from the road were small tables and chairs, some of them occupied. They sat beneath a great chestnut tree, heavy with pink blooms, and Meral's mother ordered for them all. They were given tea, brought in a big copper samovar. When a spigot was turned, the hot tea filled the glass set under it. There were little china saucers upon which to set their glasses, and lemon and sugar to flavor the tea.

At the next table a Turkish gentleman sat contentedly smoking the strangest pipe Vicki had ever seen. It was a *narghile*, Meral said, and had a very long coiled tube which drew the smoke through a fat base that held water.

"Like the caterpillar smoking a hookah in *Alice's Adventures in Wonderland*," said Adria.

This place, Meral explained, was near the former palace of the sultan's sister, where her great-grandmother had once been a lady-in-waiting. The gardens were still there, though the palace was gone. If they liked, she would show them the terraces on the way home.

Adria went suddenly dreamy and thoughtful, and Vicki guessed she was thinking of Leyla's spells again. A palace—and gardens. It did not matter that the palace was gone. Leyla had mentioned only the gardens. Vicki's old uneasiness about Adria returned to set a damper upon these happy moments.

Later they drove past weed-grown levels encased in walls of stone that climbed the hill. Long ago lovely fruit trees and flower beds had graced the palace garden, where Queen Anne's lace now reigned informally. The pool was still visible, empty and strewn with rubble.

They did not stop at this sad place but drove home. There Nursel *hanimefendi* thanked them warmly in Turkish for helping Meral today. Soon they must come and visit Meral's home across the Bosporus, she said. Vicki felt happier than she had in a long while as she and Adria went into the house.

How unfortunate that such happiness had to evaporate so quickly.

Mrs. Byrne was waiting for them, sitting on a bench in the stone-floored room. One look at her expression and the warm feeling died right out of Vicki. She felt Adria's fingers close about her arm and hold on tight, as if she too braced herself for whatever was to come.

"I thought you'd be home sooner," Mrs. Byrne said. "Ken came in sometime ago, though your father hasn't returned."

"Meral's mother took us to tea," Vicki said. "We told Dad we'd be late. But I guess he's late too this afternoon."

Mrs. Byrne did not answer. She walked to the door of the sitting room and flung it open.

"Come here!" she said.

In dread Vicki approached the door. Adria came with her, and she heard the sharp intake of her breath as they looked into the room. It took only a glance to see what had happened.

Every one of the items in Mrs. Byrne's collection had been removed from the glass cabinet and set in a long, serpentine line winding across the floor. Ivory monkeys marched behind satsuma bowls, elephants behind a Buddha of brass. Every small article was there in that curving line.

"Well?" Mrs. Byrne said. "What have you two to say about this?"

Neither girl spoke. Vicki found that her lips had gone dry, and she did not dare to look at Adria.

"Which one of you thought up this little joke?" Mrs. Byrne persisted.

Both girls were silent, and still they did not look at each other.

"Perhaps I should put it in a different way," Mrs. Byrne said. "Suppose you tell me which one of you did not do this."

Again complete silence met her words. Because of Adria, Vicki couldn't speak out. But this was too much. Adria had gone too far, and Vicki could not bear to look at her.

"I'm glad now that I wrote to Hinton Brace," Mrs. Byrne went on. "Since neither of you will speak, I can only suppose you are in this together."

"Would you like us to put the things back in the cabinet?" Vicki asked in a faint voice.

Mrs. Byrne shook her head indignantly. "Indeed, I would not. And I'm afraid, Vicki, that the time has come when I'll have to tell your father about your taking my little pin and losing it. Hinton will have to decide what is to be done about Adria, but it's for your father to deal with you."

Adria made a small movement toward Mrs. Byrne, and Vicki knew she meant to speak out. She put a hand on her arm and squeezed hard, willing her to be still. This wasn't the time—not yet. Not with all this new trouble staring them in the face.

Mrs. Byrne turned her back and began to pick up her collection piece by piece, replacing the articles on the glass shelves. Vicki knew they had been dismissed, and she tugged at Adria's elbow. Together they went out of the room and hurried for the stairs. Adria pulled herself free and ran ahead, reaching her own door before Vicki could stop her. With a resounding slam she closed it in Vicki's face, and she would not answer when Vicki called to her.

Ken heard the sound and came out of his room. "Let her alone," he said. "She's going to get exactly what's coming to her, but you don't have to be mixed up in it."

"I am mixed up in it," Vicki said quietly. Strangely enough, this was true, though not in the way Ken meant. Just as it was true that she had been mixed up in Meral's affairs this afternoon, she was involved all through this adventure with Adria. "She's still my friend," she added. "I can't get away from that. I don't think I want to."

"Anyway, leave her alone now," Ken said. He led the way into the big salon and walked to the chess table. "Mom showed me what happened. I didn't tell her, but the same trick was played on me. When I got up this morning, all my chessmen were set out in a marching line, single file across the floor here. You can't tell me you were the one to play a trick like that."

"Adria was away in school all day," Vicki said miserably. "How could she have a chance to touch those things in your mother's downstairs room?"

"Mom didn't go into the room until this afternoon, so it could have been done late last night, or early this morning. I kept still about my chess set because there's trouble enough as it is."

"Yes," Vicki said dully, "there's trouble enough." The words from *Pinafore* that she had heard that afternoon ran through her mind: *"Say, why is everything either at sixes or at sevens?"*

"Listen!" said Ken abruptly, and motioned toward the stair well.

Voices reached them from downstairs. Mrs. Byrne's voice, raised and indignant, then the quieter voice of a man. Ken's mother had lost no time. She was showing Dad what had happened, and she was undoubtedly telling him about the lost pin and the role she believed Vicki to have played in taking it.

The Turkish bracelet felt tight on Vicki's arm, and she slipped it down to her wrist, slid her hand through without unclasping it. The bracelet was, in a way, an award of merit. She must remember that. No matter what Mrs. Byrne said or her father thought right now, these things weren't important. Because she wasn't guilty. As soon as Adria was straightened out and saved from the foolish predicaments into which she threw herself in such headlong fashion, then the truth could be told and everything explained.

Ken heard her father coming up the stairs, and he gave her a sympathetic look before slipping away. Standing in the middle of that huge salon with its great polished floor, its scattered prayer rugs and pieces of furniture, its high ceiling and tall arched windows, Vicki felt smaller and more helpless than she had ever felt in her life before.

Her father's steps were slow, and she saw the discouraged set of his shoulders as he came up the stairs. She waited for him in the center of the big room.

When he saw her, he looked at her sadly. "I'm sorry, Vicki, but I'm afraid I must send you home. I thought your coming here might work out, but I can see now that it won't. Your mother won't be well enough to travel for months, and I can't handle this without her. There will be some camp we can put you in until Aunt May gets home from her trip."

He did not wait for her to speak but walked away. Holding the bracelet tightly in her hand, Vicki went to her room and closed the door softly behind her.

# 17

# The Ninth Stone

Vicki did not stir from her room for the rest of that day. She did not want to see anyone, or talk to anyone. Not even to Ken. No one requested her presence at dinner and after a time the Turkish maid brought up a tray and tried to coax her to eat something. From what attempts the girl made in broken English, Vicki gathered that Adria was ill and had gone to bed.

It was the longest evening Vicki had ever spent. She ate what she could of dinner and then put the tray outside her door. The food rested heavily in her stomach. Once she went out on the veranda and leaned on the rail, watching night come up from Asia across the Bosporus. The mosques and minarets were being swallowed by darkness, the cypress groves were already black.

Her thoughts churned futilely, and she seemed able to make no plans or think of any action. Her father was against her—and without a fair hearing. She did not want to explain anything to him now. In fact, she did not care whether she ever explained. She had been sent to Turkey in disgrace, and now she would be sent home in disgrace. Aunt Laura would say "I told you so," at the first opportunity. And Mother in the hospital would be sick with further worry.

Camp? That had been denied her, and how it would be too late to join her friends, even if she wanted to. You had to sign up early, and there was always a waiting list. She would have to go to some strange place where she would know no one, have no friends. Besides—what would happen now to Adria March?

She did not rest well during the night, but by the time morning came, she was fast asleep and stayed in bed right through breakfast time.

When she opened her eyes, she knew, even before she was awake enough to remember, that something unhappy and discouraging awaited her. Everything swept back like a smothering blanket of trouble. First of all there was Adria. She wished she had been awake early enough to see her before she went to school. She must talk to Adria. The thought of waiting till late afternoon made her impatient. Something must be done, though she didn't know what.

She went downstairs and out to the kitchen. The cook let her sit at a table whose top was a great slab of fine marble. There she ate her late breakfast. The maid was fixing a tray and when Vicki asked who it was for, she learned the Adria was still sick and had stayed home from school.

"Let me take the tray to her," she offered and Fatma gave it up to her willingly. Mrs. Byrne had gone to market, so Vicki carried the tray to Adria's room without being noticed.

She knocked at her door and waited, but nothing happened. When a louder knock still brought no response, she pushed the door open and carried in the tray. Adria's bed was unmade, and Adria was not in it.

Vicki set the tray down and looked carefully about the room. Adria's school uniform hung neatly on its hanger, her maroon school jacket was in place. So she had not gone to school. Leaving the tray where it was, Vicki ran downstairs and out into the garden. But though she searched its recesses hurriedly and called Adria's name again and again, she found no one. Somehow she had not expected to. A certainty was growing at the back of her mind that Adria had played another trick. She was not sick at all, and Vicki had a good idea of where she had probably gone.

It seemed as though she had done nothing but run after

Adria ever since she had come to Turkey, she thought angrily. Now it must be done again—though she promised herself this would be the last time. Certainly this time everything must be done with the greatest of care so as to create no more difficulties. She wrote a note to Mrs. Byrne, explaining where she was going and why. Then she went downstairs and left it with the maid.

She had money in her pocket for bus fare, and she hurried down the steep road past Rumeli Hisar. Fortunately, a bus was not long in coming. She boarded it and sat where she could watch the land side. She had no idea of the name of the place where she wanted to go, but she knew she would recognize it. If Adria was not there, then nothing much had been lost, and she would go home at once. But if she knew Adria, there was little doubt of where she would find her.

The distance was short, and the palace gardens were easy to see. Vicki let the driver know she wanted to get off, and when the bus stopped she hopped down to the road and stood looking up. Scrubby grass that had once been a lawn came down to the road, and back a little way high stone terraces like steep steps went straight up the hillside. Wisteria overhung the highest wall and weeds filled the gardens. Where ladies of the court had walked in secluded beauty, traffic went noisily by and the palace on the Bosporus was gone.

Anxiously, Vicki stood at the foot of the gardens, her gaze searching each terrace in turn. There was no one there, no Adria in sight. The knot of anxiety she could feel in the pit of her stomach seemed to curl itself a notch tighter. She had been so sure Adria would be here. So sure that she would be in time to bring her back before anything more serious happened. Perhaps get her home before Mrs. Byrne returned and found them both gone.

Anyone who stood on one of those terraces would have been in clear sight—there was no place to hide. And no one was there. So there was nothing to do but admit defeat and catch the next bus home. Still—there was one other place to look. She remembered the shallow pool around which palace ladies had once gathered. It would be out of sight from where she stood—behind the lower end of the terrace wall.

She ran to the place and stood looking down. Upon a little hummock of grass sat Adria, staring at the empty pool. Her back was to the road, and she had not seen Vicki. Anger began to pound in Vicki's ears and she walked quickly, firmly toward the girl beside the pool.

Adria heard her step and looked around. She regarded Vicki without surprise and without welcome.

"I might have known," she said. "Why can't you ever mind your own business?"

This was so wildly unfair that Vicki had to take several deep breaths before she could speak.

"I'm going to be sent home," she said. "Don't you think that makes the things you've done my business?"

Adria didn't answer. Her hair still hung down her back in its nighttime braids, straggly and unbrushed. She must have come straight here the minute she could dress and slip out of the house.

"Well?" said Vicki coldly. "Did you find what you came to look for?"

Adria moved her head in a negative answer. "I haven't looked yet. I—I was afraid to."

"Afraid to?" Vicki echoed. "I didn't think you had sense enough to be afraid of anything."

With a quick motion Adria raised her head and there was no bright sea green in her eyes this morning. Unexpectedly, she seemed forlorn and ready to plead.

"If it's not there, I don't know what to do next," she said. "This is my last chance to find something to help me out of trouble. If Leyla's charm doesn't work, there's nothing left."

"There's *you* left," Vicki said sharply, the sound of anger exploding into her voice. "To get out of trouble, you might try doing things differently. You might stop being sneaky and playing tricks and making people angry with you."

"The way you're angry now," Adria said sadly. "But how does a person stop once she gets started? I don't know how to stop."

"The way to stop is to do something different!" said Vicki. But she knew what Adria meant. When things started going wrong, it was often hard to do an about-face and move in the opposite direction. It was a little like running down a hill and not being able to stop, even though you wanted to go the other way.

"I did try," Adria said. "Haven't you noticed how good I've been? And it wasn't any use. None at all. I'm going to be turned over to Uncle Hinton, and he'll put me in a school someplace and forget all about me. I know he will."

"Then why did you play that silly trick with Mrs. Byrne's collection?" Vicki demanded. "If you didn't want her to be still angrier with you, then why—"

Adria raised her head, staring. "*I* play a trick with that collection? I never touched her old things at all. I never set foot in that sitting room. I thought it was you. That's why I kept still. You haven't been keeping out of trouble very well yourself, you know."

The two girls looked at each other blankly for a moment.

"You mean it wasn't you?" Vicki said in disbelief.

"Of course it wasn't! All I want is to find Leyla's charm and keep out of trouble for the rest of my life."

Vicki refrained from pointing out that pretending to be sick and sneaking out of the house like this were not the best ways in the world to change things for the better. Her attention was still upon one thing.

"I didn't take Mrs. Byrne's things out of her cabinet either," she said. "So who could it have been?"

Adria shrugged. "Ken, I suppose. Boys like to play jokes, and besides, he doesn't like me. He'd enjoy being rid of me for good."

Vicki found it hard to believe that Ken had done so mean a thing. Surely he wouldn't tamper with his mother's collection. Still—it had been very carefully done. Nothing had been broken, and if he wanted to make certain that Adria would not go home to the States with the Byrnes, he could hardly have found a better way.

Nevertheless, she shook her head. "I don't think he'd do a thing like that."

"We can't solve it now," Adria said and stood up. "I feel braver with you here, Victoria. Come with me. Let's go up there and search."

It was better for Adria to get this notion out of her mind and done with forever, Vicki supposed, walking with her to the foot of the terraces.

Adria looked up at the mounting stone walls. "Three up, the message said. There are four terraces, so we stop one before the top. Come along—there are steps over at the side."

The stones were crumbling, and they had to climb carefully. Burrs caught at their legs and skirts and reached out to snag Adria's long braids. Something of Adria's excitement reached out to touch Vicki too. She did not believe in gypsy spells, but Leyla had stopped being quite so mysterious at the end and had given Mrs. Byrne specific directions.

They were on the third terrace now, and Adria was studying the vine-covered wall. "Nine stones to the right, Leyla said. That was it, wasn't it?"

"That's what Mrs. Byrne told you," Vicki admitted. "But I don't know which row of stones you're supposed to count. With all that overgrowth I don't see how you can count nine of anything."

Thick vines—perhaps vines that had once been a grape arbor—hung over the terrace, hiding the stones from sight. Adria was not to be daunted. She thrust her hands into the dusty vines and began to feel beneath them. Then she turned to Vicki, her eyes alive with excitement.

"Look—the vines are loose! Someone has pulled them away from the wall so that they're hanging like a curtain. Help me push them up."

Together they lifted the vines and tossed a section up over the terrace above. Now the top stones of the wall were revealed and Adria began to count, touching each stone with her hand. Vicki counted with her, holding her breath.

"Nine to the right—this is the one!" Adria cried. She

put her hand on a big moss-covered stone and pushed it back and forth. "It rocks," she said, and drew her hand away.

"Well, go ahead," Vicki urged. "What are you waiting for?"

Now that she had reached her goal, Adria seemed frightened again. "You do it," she pleaded.

Vicki understood. From Adria's viewpoint, this was the end of her road. If the gypsy fortune did not help, she knew nothing else to try. That was foolish, of course, but it was the way Adria felt.

Vicki put both hands on the stone and rocked it back and forth. It came loose easily, and she lifted it from its place in the wall. Behind was a hollow that had been dug into the earthen bank. Vicki reached in and felt something smooth and slippery beneath her fingers. Fumbling now in her own rising excitement, she drew out a little packet wrapped round and round with a thin plastic covering. This was for Adria to open, and Vicki held it out to her.

"Leyla knew," Adria said softly. "She really was telling my fortune."

"Leyla is the one who put it here, whatever it is," Vicki said. "Hurry and open it."

Adria took the box and held it lightly on her palm, as though it might possess some magic life of its own. Then she glanced about at what was no more than the ghost of old palace gardens.

"Let's go down and sit beside the pool," she said. "It's warm and sunny there. I'm awfully cold."

Adria was still postponing the moment, Vicki thought impatiently. If the matter had been up to her, she would have had the box open by now. But she made no objection, and Adria led the way down a flight of crumbling stone steps that descended toward the empty basin of the pool. There they sat upon a grassy bank between pool and road and at last Adria removed the cover of the box. Within was a padding of cotton. She drew out the top layer and gasped. Eagerly Vicki leaned forward to look. There, nested in cotton, lay a tiny golden horn in the shape of Istanbul's Golden Horn.

"It's Mrs. Byrne's pin!" Vicki cried in delight. She could not have felt happier or more surprised. Now the pin could be returned, and Mrs. Byrne would be pleased and perhaps forgiving. Even Dad might feel better about everything and reconsider his own decision.

It was the expression on Adria's face that brought Vicki back to earth. Adria had taken the pin from its nest of cotton and was holding it on the palm of her hand. Her eyes were filled with tears.

"What's the matter?" Vicki demanded. "You couldn't find anything that could help us more."

Adria only shook her head. "Leyla said a golden horn—something that would bring me good fortune and make nice things happen to me. Giving Mrs. Byrne her pin now isn't going to do any of those things. It isn't a *real* fortune. It's only something Leyla did to help her made-up fortune come true."

Vicki picked up the empty box. Something showed beneath the bottom layer of cotton, and she pulled out a small folded square of paper. When she opened it she found that words had been printed upon it in large, uncertain letters.

The two girls read the message together:

"Cemile takes pin. I do not know. I find in toys.
Is no time to return. I tell to lady where pin is hide."

That was all, but they could guess the rest.

"I can see how she must have figured," Vicki said. "When Leyla found the pin among Cemile's things, she knew it was important to get it back to you. But she was leaving town and couldn't put it into your hands herself. So she remembered the fortune she'd been making up for fun and decided to make it come true. When she saw Mrs. Byrne, the idea of getting the pin back to you this way must have come to her."

Adria nodded gloomy agreement. "Gypsies are always hiding things outdoors and leaving signs for one another, so I expect you're right. She wouldn't have had it with her to give Mrs. Byrne at the time. And this would seem sensible to her. If I didn't understand and find the pin, it would still be safe until the next time she returned to Istanbul."

"You said gypsies wouldn't steal from a friend," Vicki reminded her.

"I don't think you could call it stealing with someone as young as Cemile. She must have seen it there in the grass and picked it up because it caught her eye. And Leyla didn't know she had it. Anyway, that's the end of our fortunetelling. I suppose I've been the foolish one all along."

She put the pin into the box and got slowly to her feet. Without speaking, the two girls went down to the road together. When the next bus came along, they boarded it and not until they left it near Rumeli Hisar and started the climb toward home, did either one find anything to say. Vicki was waiting for Adria to suggest the next step, but when she did not, she finally put her own ideas into words.

"Let's give the pin to Mrs. Byrne as soon as she comes back from market. Let's tell her the whole story."

Adria shook her head. "You're always saying that I jump into things without thinking. Now I want to think about this. I want to do it the best way. Instead of giving the pin to Cousin Janet, perhaps we could show it to your father first."

"To Dad?" Vicki was surprised.

"Yes. He always seems just and kind. It might be better if he told Cousin Janet the story, instead of our trying to. She's so awfully mad at us that she might not want to listen."

Vicki glanced in surprise at the girl climbing the hill beside her. "Do you think my father is kind and just?" she asked.

"Of course I do," said Adria. "I've never seen him lose his temper, no matter how you act."

"How *I* act!" Vicki began to sputter. "How can you say that when he never gave me a chance to explain last night? He went off in that silence he pulls around him and didn't come near me all evening."

"Because you tie yourself in a knot and resist him with

all your might," Adria said. "I've seen you do it. He must think there's no use talking to you then, and probably he's right."

Indignation made Vicki stammer. "I n-n-never heard of such a thing! He's not like other fathers. At home most dads are pals with their kids. My father's never been like that. He talks more to the girls in his classes than he does to me."

"Hey—wait a minute!" Adria cried. "Let's sit down and talk a minute before we go back to the house."

There was a low stone wall beside the road and while Vicki did not feel she had much to talk about, she sat upon it beside Adria and stared into the branches of a flowering Judas tree.

"Maybe gifted people are like that sometimes," Adria said. "Off in a world where we can't always follow. My father was that way quite often. Mother used to say we had to be glad he was someone special and not ask him to be exactly like everybody else."

Vicki heard her in some surprise. Always Adria could be counted on for the unexpected. So often she was imaginative in an almost childish way. Yet the next moment she could see matters in a manner that was thoughtful and almost grown up. Before Vicki could find an answer, Adria jumped down from the wall and stood facing her.

"Don't you know how lucky you are to have a father, Victoria?" she cried.

Then she turned and began to walk quickly up the hill. Vicki went with her, and after a few steps she slipped her hand through the crook of Adria's elbow and they walked home in a silence that was somehow understanding and thoroughly companionable.

# 18

# Gift of the Golden Horn

Mrs. Byrne was not yet home, and Vicki retreived her note and tore it up. Later the whole story would be told, but not yet. She was willing to follow Adria's suggestion and tell Dad the whole thing first.

At lunchtime Adria came down from her room and said she would go back to school for the afternoon. Mrs. Byrne continued to be distant and disapproving through the whole meal, but that did not matter so much, because in a little while a lot of things could be explained and made right.

During the afternoon Vicki was seized by an inspiration. She went to work on a special drawing for Adria. It was a different sort of golden horn—a cornucopia, the "horn of plenty." Instead of filling the horn's mouth with the luscious fruits of mythology, she drew small, interesting shapes spilling out of it. She placed no labels upon them, since her growing feeling about Adria's worth could not be pinned down and labeled. Adria would either know what she meant—or she wouldn't. Anyway, the moment had not yet come to give her the drawing.

When Dad came home from school, bringing Ken and Adria with him, it was Vicki who found the courage to ask for a chance to talk to him. He nodded gravely, and Vicki slipped a hand through Adria's arm, drawing her into the conference.

"Only the three of us," Vicki said. "Someplace where we can talk by ourselves."

Her father agreed. "I've been wanting this," he said. "I spoke too quickly last night. I'm afraid I wasn't fair."

Vicki was surprised by the surge of affection for her father that went through her. She had not been fair either.

The three went into the garden where plane trees spread the shade of late afternoon over the warm tiles of the fountain. Dad sat on the marble bench nearby, while the two girls seated themselves cross-legged on the grass before him. Dad did not wait for Vicki to indicate what she wanted to discuss. He started right in himself.

"I had a letter from your mother today," he told his daughter. "It was a long, very revealing letter. She wants you to forgive her for writing to me about these matters first. She'll answer your letter later. She told me the whole story of the pin, Vicki, just as you told it to her. I'm relieved, and I'm sorry too. I wish you'd told me all this yourself though I can see how you felt you must protect Adria. Perhaps some of the fault is mine. I was busy with my work and probably didn't give you much chance to confide in me. I'm sure Mrs. Byrne would have understood if the whole story had been told her at once."

Adria began to shake her head, and Vicki could wait no longer.

"We've found the pin!" she cried. "Leyla put it in a secret place because there was no time to bring it here. Show it to him, Adria!"

Adria took the box from her pocket and opened it for Dad to see. His expression told them how pleased he was. He had intended, he said, to give Mother's letter to Mrs. Byrne anyway. Now, if they liked, he would tell her the rest of the story as well.

"You both owe her some very big apologies that you'll have to manage yourselves," he added.

Adria had listened soberly. She rose with the little box held tightly in her hand. "I made all the trouble," she said. "So it's up to me to get something right. I'll go now and tell Cousin Janet what happened, and about how Victoria was protecting me and—and everything." She did not wait to hear what they thought but walked quickly away toward the house.

*And everything*, Vicki thought. Would that include what had happened to Mrs. Byrne's collection yesterday? There was still an unanswered mystery there, even though Adria had tried to place the blame on Ken.

"Come and sit beside me, young Miss Victoria," Dad said. He was looking at her as though he really saw her and approved of what he saw.

Vicki seated herself a little shyly on the marble bench.

"There was more in that letter from Mother," he said. "She is feeling much better—that's the most important thing of all. The doctor thinks she may be able to join us out here in another six weeks or so."

Join them? Then Dad had changed his mind about sending her home, Vicki thought, too happy over her mother and this new thought to be able to speak.

"She wrote about Adria too," Dad went on. "But these are things we must not tell Adria right now. We'll have to wait and see. You know how close Adria's mother and your mother were when they were young. They kept in touch after they were grown up, even though they hadn't seen each other for such a long while. Because of this feeling, your mother would like to help Adria. If it's possible. When she comes out here, she's going to see how we all get along together and how she feels when she gets to know Adria. It's possible we might keep her with us here in Turkey for a visit, and see how it worked out. Later— who knows?"

Vicki's eyes were shining. "You mean we might take her into our family? Bring her home with us?"

"Don't go too fast," Dad said. "This is something that will have to grow. In the meantime, not a word of this must be hinted to Adria. The disappointment would be too great if we had to decide against keeping her with us."

"But, Dad—" Vicki said anxiously, "if Adria knew what you're considering, then she'd be sure to—to do things the right way, and—"

He shook his head rather sternly. "Not a word, Vicki. Do you promise me that?"

There was nothing else to do. She promised and knew she was bound to secrecy. Still, she now had something big to hope for as far as Adria was concerned. This would give Adria a chance to stay in Turkey a while longer. And Vicki suspected that she would not mind going to America so much if she knew she would be going there with the Stewarts.

"Adria has to get off on a new foot by herself," Dad went on. "You can help, but you can't do it for her. Any more than someone else can do it for you now that you've decided to apply that very good mind of yours and make up your schoolwork."

So Mother had told him that too. Vicki wasn't entirely sure she approved of his tone or of her mother telling. The old feeling of resistance began to rise in her.

"Don't you know how proud of you I am?" he said gently.

She looked at him in surprise. "How can you be proud when I'm not going to pass in school, and—"

"I'm proud because you've learned what to do with failure. How to turn it inside out and use it for the helpful tool it is. Don't you think I had to learn that too, Vicki? And more than once in my life, as everyone must. It comes to us in different ways, but it's always the same thing."

She wasn't sure she understood what he meant, and he must have seen her uncertainty because he went on.

"How did you feel about good marks in the past?" he asked.

She thought for a moment. "Oh, pleased, I guess."

"And how will you feel about your next good marks, honey?"

How would she feel? It wasn't possible to explain exactly, because the very thought of being up near the top of the class, gave her such a sense of tingling elation that it couldn't be put into words. But there was one thing she could say with all her heart.

"I'll feel as though I'd earned them," she told him.

He smiled. "You'll be right too. Failure is pretty useful to us when we turn it into a steppingstone. You needn't regret it, Vicki."

When they walked back to the house together, his arm

was about her shoulders, and she had never felt so close to her father.

By dinnertime, since Adria had seen her own difficult task through and Mrs. Byrne had her pin again, everyone's spirits were bubbling over. At the table only Ken, who still did not know the story, watched them in bewilderment. When his mother explained about the return of the pin, he listened soberly and did not join in the conversation with the others. His lack of enthusiasm worried Vicki, and after dinner she managed to catch him alone.

"What's the matter?" she asked. "Everything's cleared up. Why aren't you cheerful about it?"

He tried an unsuccessful grin. "Maybe I'm just an old cynic," he said. "But I don't believe all this about Adria reforming and staying out of trouble. Maybe it's only a hunch, Vicki, but there's one thing I know."

"What's that?" Vicki asked impatiently.

"Nothing is going to happen tonight," Ken said. "Nothing is going wrong because I'm going to see that it doesn't."

She laughed aloud in his face and told him how silly he was being. He didn't understand Adria as she did.

That evening the two girls had a companionable time studying together. Dad said he would write and get the proper make-up work for Vicki, but it wouldn't hurt to study with Adria for now.

That night there was no lying awake. Vicki knew, if Ken didn't, that Adria was out of the foolish corner she had painted herself into, and nothing more was going to happen. Though she had to admit that by now she wasn't entirely sure of Ken. She remembered the accusation Adria had made. She had not paid much attention to it at the time, but what if Ken's gloom grew out of his own guilty conscience? Or what if he was worried lest his mother reconsider and take Adria home with them after all?

During the night rain began to fall. The sound of it against window panes and on the veranda outside her room wakened Vicki. She did not mind. It was a light, almost tuneful sound, and she felt peaceful and content listening to it. The rain was lulling her back to sleep when a creaking on the stairs brought her suddenly wide awake. The old house creaked a good deal in the night, but this had been a louder sound than usual. At once she was awake and fearful.

She got out of bed and ran to the door. She opened it a crack and peered across the dimly lighted salon. She was in time to see the flicker of Adria's white dress as she sped up the stairs and into the far hall. Her door opened and shut in the flicker of an eyelash, and everything was still except for the soft sound of rain falling on the roof.

Oh, no! Vicki thought. Not again. Not more trouble. She couldn't bear it if Adria had played some new trick that would spoil everything. But she had to know; she had to find out.

Quickly she slipped on her bathrobe and slippers and went into the hall. At least no one else seemed to have heard the creaking of the stairs. Her slippers had sponge rubber soles and made no sound at all, except when her weight pressed a sigh from some aging board.

Softly she crept down the stairs, cold now with a rising dread. Cold as she had been that night Adria had rescued her in the haremlik. At the foot of the stairs, a dim light burned. All was still and undisturbed. The door of the Turkish sitting room stood closed. Hating what she must do, more fearful than ever, she crossed the stone floor. The door was ajar a mere crack, and it opened without a sound. Inside all was pitch dark.

Her fingers found the light switch near the door, and yellow light swept across the room. She stood on the doorsill, staring in despair at a serpentine trail that led across the room. Mrs. Byrne's collection, placed neatly one piece after another in winding single file, was on the march again.

How *could* Adria have repeated this trick? What could she possibly hope to gain when things had been going so well?

A faint sound across the room startled her and for the first time Vicki looked beyond the marching line upon the floor. The sound had been a snore. There on a low Turkish divan lay Kenneth Byrne, fast asleep and breathing through his open mouth. He was dressed in slacks and a sweater, but he was cold enough to have drawn himself into a tight ball.

Vicki crossed the room and shook him by one shoulder. He snorted and tried to turn over, but she kept on shaking until he opened his eyes and looked up at her. Then he seemed to realize where he was and sat up to swing his feet to the floor. At once the marching array of his mother's collection met his eyes, and he gaped at it, coming fully awake.

"Did you do that, Vicki?" he asked in dismay.

"Of course I didn't," Vicki said. "And I don't think you did either. But why are you down here?"

He stood up and stretched widely, sounding sheepish as he answered. "I meant to watch. I thought I'd hear if anyone came into the room. But I didn't hear a thing. I guess I never stirred at all. I'd sure never make a good detective!"

He flapped his arms about himself, trying to warm up.

"You should have brought a blanket," Vicki commented absently. She knew what the next move must be, though she hated to make it.

"I did bring a blanket," Ken said and looked around the room in bewilderment. "Good night—she took that too. Right off me while I was asleep!"

"She?" Vicki repeated helplessly.

"Of course," he said. "Who else? Do you think I swallowed all that lovey-dovey stuff at dinner tonight? A person like Adria doesn't change that fast. But now the blanket will prove she was down here. Come along, Vicki. We've got to see this through and end it for good."

She knew there was nothing else to do and when he hurried toward the stairs, she followed, heavy hearted. She did not tell him she had seen Adria. What they would find must speak for itself.

"Don't knock," Ken whispered. "Open the door and go right in. Turn on the light before she can hide anything."

Somehow her feet and her hands managed to obey her. She stopped before Adria's door, with Ken behind her, opened it, and felt for the switch. Once more a room sprang brightly alive in the glow of electricity.

Adria was in bed and under the covers. She sat up at once as though she had not been asleep and gave a little squeal of fright. Vicki cast a quick glance about the room and saw the white dress on a chair where she had flung it.

"Where's the blanket?" Ken demanded in a whisper from the doorway. "Where did you hide it?"

Adria only stared at him.

"I—I saw you on the stairs," Vicki admitted miserably. "I saw your white dress. And we found all the things on the floor again."

"You needn't have swiped the blanket and left me cold," Ken told her.

Adria shook her head from side to side as though she were shaking it free of sleep.

"I had an awful dream," she said. "I dreamed that the harem ladies were angry with me and meant to burn the house down over our heads. I dreamed they were all out and moving around in the halls. When I heard one at my door, I woke up. But it was only you."

"Don't pull that stuff with us," Ken said. "We've caught you this time. Maybe we'd better go talk to Mom right now, without waiting till morning."

Adria moved fast. She slid out of bed, flung on her bathrobe over her pajamas, and opened a bureau drawer.

"I've had enough of ghosts," she said and when she turned around, she had a flashlight in her hand. "I have a strong suspicion. Come along, both of you."

When she went into the hall, moving softly now, the other two followed. Ken muttered under his breath, but he walked as softly as Adria and Vicki.

"What are you going to do?" Vicki asked.

Adria didn't bother to answer. She went straight to the big carved door that shut off the harem wing and opened it. Her flashlight beam cut through the darkness, showing nothing but an extension of the long bare hall that led to the big salon at the far end. Nothing had changed; nothing was revealed. But Adria continued to move purposefully.

With determined thoroughness, she went to each closed door in turn, opened it, and sent her flashlight beam around the room's emptiness, then went on to the next door.

"How silly can you be?" Ken said. "You don't think you can get out of this by hunting for ghosts, do you?"

"I'm not hunting for ghosts," Adria said. She flung open the fourth door, and Vicki, close behind, felt her stiffen. "There!" cried Adria. "Look there!"

They stared in bewilderment. Across the room in a corner lay a blanket-wrapped bundle. It seemed at first to have neither head nor feet, but at the slap of Adria's Turkish slippers on the floor, it wriggled and a pair of bright black eyes peered out over the blanket's edge.

Adria pounced, reaching for an arm, pulling the bundle to its feet. "Get up, Cemile!" she cried. "Get up and tell us what you're doing here."

The tousled head and make-shift clothes of the gypsy child emerged in the beam of light. She blinked and began to sob into the crook of her arm. At once Adria set the light down and knelt beside the little girl, her arms around her gently.

"Don't cry, Cemile. It's wonderful that you're not lost. But don't you realize how heartbroken Leyla is? We must find a way to let her know you're all right and get you back to her."

"No, no!" Cemile cried. In a mingling of Turkish and English she poured out her story. "I want to be like you, *Küçük Hanim,*" she told Adria. "To read the books and live in house. I do not want to be gypsy. Leyla wants. I do not want. I run away and am walking here. It takes many days, but kind people give me food. To be like Amer-i-kan girl is how I wish. I hide here, and Leyla goes away."

Her English was better than Leyla's, but now she burst into a flood of Turkish, clinging to Adria with both arms around her neck.

Ken began to laugh, and Vicki smiled in relief.

"Ask her why she played that trick with Mom's things," Ken said.

Cemile understood. "Adria makes the funny trick. At Grandmother's house she tells to me about trick with tools in workshop. Is very funny. So I make funny trick too in night." She had forgotten her tears, and her small face was alight with mischief. "Nobody catch," she added.

"Somebody did catch," Ken corrected. "It was you who took my blanket, wasn't it?"

"Is cold," said Cemile simply.

Adria stood up and moved the flashlight beam around the room to reveal how this particular little ghost had been living for nearly two days in their midst. There was evidence of food brought from the kitchen, of water and fruit, and a book from Adria's room. A dress of Adria's hung neatly on a nail.

"You do not wake up tonight," Cemile said to Adria, laughing a little. "I look in dresses and get white dress for wearing. But is very long. So when I come upstairs I bring a different one."

Ken stopped smiling and looked straight at Adria. "I'm sorry," he said in honest apology. "I was sure it was you all along."

"How could I blame you?" Adria said. "It doesn't matter now. What are we to do about Cemile?"

Since discovering the gypsy child, they had forgotten to whisper and their louder voices must have gone echoing through the house. Vicki heard the footsteps first and waved to the others to be quiet. Mrs. Byrne was up and so was Dad, and they were coming down the hall. Adria's flashlight showed the two adults in the doorway, staring in sleepy astonishment at the scene before them.

"We've caught our mouse," Ken said, indicating Cemile.

It was Dad who suggested that they all go back to the lighted area of the house and start the charcoal brazier— since it looked as if they might be up for a while straightening things out.

In the salon they lighted lamps and drew chairs about the big brass *mangal*. Rain whispered softly in the background while Ken and Adria and Vicki all told parts of the story. Cemile, with Ken's blanket wrapped around her, huddled close to Adria and listened round-eyed, less impudent now, a little awed by the presence of American grownups who held her fate in their hands.

"What are we to do with the child?" Mrs. Byrne sighed when the story was told. "How are we to find her sister with a traveling gypsy tribe? We can't keep her here."

"Tomorrow we can take her back to her grandparents," Adria said. "They will be happy to keep her from being a gypsy. In Istanbul she can go to school as she wants to do. Leyla will have to understand that her little sister must have a chance to do what is best for her. I think Leyla won't mind so much, once she knows she isn't lost after all. But Cemile needs to be a Turkish girl, not an American."

No matter how late the hour, Mrs. Byrne insisted that Cemile must have a bath and discard those oversized clothes. Then a cot was set up for her in Adria's room and the warm, sleepy little gypsy who did not want to be a gypsy, was bedded down in it.

There were "good nights" all around and no one worried because Mrs. Byrne's collection would march in a weaving line for the rest of the night.

Back in her room, Vicki knew she had one more thing to do. She waited till Dad and Mrs. Byrne had gone to their rooms. Then she got what she wanted from her bureau and once more ventured out into the cold hall. At Adria's door she made the scratching sound that the other girl had used as a signal to her the first night she was here.

"Come in," Adria called softly.

The light was still on. Tiptoeing into the room, Vicki saw that Adria was in bed again. On the cot Cemile lay sound asleep, her hair damp and curly from the steamy bath.

"I brought you something," Vicki said and found herself a little hesitant. Perhaps Adria would only think her silly. Nevertheless, she held out the drawing she had made of a cornucopia.

Adria sat up and took it from her. She held the picture

to the lamplight and studied it for a few moments in silence.

"It—I—I made it for you," Vicki told her awkwardly.

Adria glanced up from the drawing, and her eyes were shining. "A golden horn!" she whispered. "And you've left places for me to fill in the things I most want. I know it will bring me good fortune."

She sat up on the edge of the bed and put her two hands on Vicki's shoulders.

"Bend down," she said. When Vicki did, Adria kissed her lightly, first on one cheek and then on the other in the Turkish fashion. "Thank you, Victoria," she said.

If she stayed a moment longer, she would cry, Vicki knew. She fled from the room, blinking hard and hurried to her own bed. The sheets were cold, but she did not mind. There was so much to think about—so many plans to make. But she was growing sleepy now and would have to put them off till tomorrow.

Perhaps everyone had a horn of plenty, she thought drowsily. And perhaps you had to put into it what you wanted to take out. Maybe it was as simple as that. And as hard.

The house slept, and the rain ceased. A widening crescent of moon came out from behind the clouds and floated like a golden horn against the deep-blue sky of the Turkish night.

## SIGNET Young Adult Titles You'll Enjoy

- [ ] **DELPHA GREEN & COMPANY by Vera and Bill Cleaver.**
(#Y6907—$1.25)
- [ ] **GROVER by Vera and Bill Cleaver.** (#Y6714—$1.25)
- [ ] **I WOULD RATHER BE A TURNIP by Vera and Bill Cleaver.** (#Y7034—$1.25)
- [ ] **ME TOO by Vera and Bill Cleaver.** (#Y6519—$1.25)
- [ ] **WHERE THE LILIES BLOOM by Vera and Bill Cleaver.**
(#W8065—$1.50)
- [ ] **I'VE MISSED A SUNSET OR THREE by Phyllis Anderson Wood.** (#Y7944—$1.25)
- [ ] **SONG OF THE SHAGGY CANARY by Phyllis Anderson Wood.** (#Y7859—$1.25)
- [ ] **YOUR BIRD IS HERE, TOM THOMPSON by Phyllis Anderson Wood.** (#Y8192—$1.25)
- [ ] **JUST WE THREE by Charlotte Herman.** (#Q6758—95¢)
- [ ] **NOTHING EVER HAPPENS HERE by Carol Beach York.**
(#Y7991—$1.25)
- [ ] **MR. AND MRS. BO JO JONES by Ann Head.**
(#W7869—$1.50)
- [ ] **MATTY DOOLIN by Catherine Cookson.**
(#Y7126—$1.25)
- [ ] **SYCAMORE YEAR by Mildred Lee.** (#Y7073—$1.25)
- [ ] **RUN, SHELLEY, RUN! by Gertrude Samuels.**
(#W7827—$1.50)
- [ ] **LIKE THE LION'S TOOTH by Marjorie Kellogg.**
(#Y5655—$1.25)

## Other SIGNET Books You Will Enjoy